Touch

Touch
A novel by Envy Red

Red Door Books

Waldorf, MD

Published by

Red Door Books

P.O. Box 668

Waldorf, MD 20604

For more information on Envy Red please visit http://envyred.com

Comments and Letters are welcome:

Envy Red

c/o Red Door Books

2351 Windsor Park Ct

Waldorf, MD 20602

Email: Envyred@envyred.com

ISBN: 978-0-578-07269-2

Library of Congress Control Number: 2010918458

This is a work of fiction. It is not intended to depict, portray, or represent any real persons or events. All of the characters are fictional and any similarities to actual events, places, or people both living and dead are only intended to give the novel a sense of reality. Other similarities are entirely coincidental.

Cover Image by Ondre Hunt

http://hunt4photos.com

Book Design and Cover Layout by Shane Cox

http://ripgraphics.com

Printed in the United States of America

To my boys

By entrusting me with your lives, god has blessed me exceedingly and abundantly. You are my constant source of inspiration and motivation. The world is your playground and the sky has no limits.

To my mom

There truly is no love like a mother's love. Thank you for your support as I journeyed to make my first novel a reality. You will always be my very own cheerleader encouraging me to push beyond my wildest dreams.

To Shane Cox

For believing in my vision and spending countless hours helping me make it a reality. Your creativity, endless advice, technical expertise, and huge heart will not be forgotten as we continue on.

To all of the cancer patients and survivors of the world

I was diagnosed as I wrote this book. It did not stop me and it won't stop you. Never give up the fight. Keep pushing forward. Your star will shine on.

"I waited patiently for the Lord; and he inclined unto me and heard my cry. He brought me up also out of a horrible pit, out of the miry clay, and set my feet upon a rock, and established my goings."

---Psalm 40:1-2

Prologue

The howling of the wind and the crack of lightening that followed could not mask the sounds of pure pain and misery that my father's beating was placing on my mother.

"Carolyn, you stupid whore I know you are messing around on me!" he screamed.

"Earl I would never do such a thing. I promise," she stuttered while spitting out blood from her freshly split lip.

"Please he was just saying hello baby I'm sorry."

"You will be you dirty cunt of a woman," he slurred.

Alcohol was his demon of choice and it constantly flowed through his veins just as pure as water. The slap that followed or her heinous scream thereafter should have cut right through the thunder and woke the neighbors but my aunt's pleading was the only sign of mercy that god was showing my mother on that stormy summer's night.

"Earl please don't do this! The children are asleep!" Aunt Vivian pleaded.

Aunt Vivi is what we called her. She was my mother's identical twin. Like my mother, she had smooth caramel skin with long jet black hair. Unlike my mother who pulled hers back in a tight bun except when washing it, and often let me brush it with her big wooden paddle brush for hours, she relaxed hers and let its length hang over her shoulders. She was always a frail petite woman standing 4'11" at best but overflowing with life.

She gave us allot of candy. Boston Baked Beans were my favorite. My brother, on the other hand, loved him some lemon heads from the bebop lady who sold everything from chips, to pickles, to shaved ice loaded with cherry/blue raspberry flavoring on top. From this special frozen treat that the neighborhood kids called "bebops," for reasons that remain a mystery, is where she got her name "bebop lady." My mother never let us eat candy so having Aunt Vivi come visit was always a joy.

While referring to herself as a city gal who happened to be born in Bama, she loved to tell us stories about life in our nation's capital Washington, DC. With nothing but go karts and dirt roads to entertain us when we visited extended family in Tarrant, we listened eagerly to her tales of shopping sprees and city living with Aunt Jennifer, the oldest of three girls and one boy. Our Uncle Eugene was the youngest and ran off to the army as soon as he was of age to escape the south. Eventually he married and settled in Washington DC where he made a military career.

They constantly pleaded with my mother to move us there. Everyone knew our family's dark secret but it was not discussed as far as I knew. My mother would always say "I'm a southern gal and the south is where I'm staying." I never had the heart to tell her that technically Washington, DC is the south. At least that's what my social studies teacher Ms. Greene told me.

Aunt Vivi was fun to have around. Besides, he never beat us when there was company so her presence was double the treat. Tonight I listened as Aunt Vivi pleaded with daddy to stop as if death were knocking and she were my mother's guardian angel sent from above.

I shivered as my little six year old brother reached out to me and climbed into my bed. I held him close.

"Don't worry it will be over soon lil one," I said. "Don't you

2

worry your big head," I continued with certainty. It was my duty to protect him. After all I am and will always be my brother's keeper.

With each roll of thunder another blow to my mother's frail body competed for its attention. I wonder what she will look like this time I couldn't help but wonder. What continent would her blackened eye be shaped after? Africa? North America? South America? Asia? All are beautiful in their own right, I thought as I watched the tears roll down my brother's face as smooth as the raindrops that slid from my window pane. Not a tear dropped from my eyes. I must be strong for him. The beating is coming to an end. It always does.

Crack!

The storm was intensifying outside and so were the screams inside the country four room shack we called home.

"Please Earl. Put the gun down you are drunk. Please don't do this. I'm calling the police!" That was my Aunt Vivi then *BOOM!*

The thunder in these parts beat down on the earth with fists of fury and was loud enough to command the same respect but that was no ordinary sound. That was the sound of eminent death cutting through the storm. Eminent is such a big word for such a young girl I remembered my teacher telling me.

My mother always told me "learn as much as you can gal and get out of here. It is home for me but the bottom is no place for such a smart girl as my baby."

"When I grow up I just want to be as beautiful as you are mama," I always replied.

To that she would say "Hush up and don't you back talk your mammy. Beauty gets you nowhere in this world. Now brains, hunny that is your key out of this hole."

I would smile and say "I know mama but I promise I will get us all out of here and away from him."

Slap!

"Don't say bad things about your daddy gal he loves us and works very hard to provide for us. He is just going through allot with the devil's juice but through the glory of god he will be healed."

The slap never stopped me from saying the same thing. Like her constant bruises, the sting would heal but the pain I felt for her

3

never would let me give in.

BOOM!

The second sound suddenly interrupted my thoughts and sent a pain through my soul that I never felt before and for a moment I thought my heart stopped.

I felt the urine ooze from my brother's super hero drawers and down his tiny legs. He always wets himself but this time was different. I couldn't even muster up the strength to yell at him. It was as if he were slowly releasing her pain through this steady flow.

The sharp smell of piss filled the room but somehow I didn't care this time. Mama would kill me if she knew I used that word. My granddaddy always said piss. I wanted to be just like him carefree. My mother said I got my sailor mouth from him and she would wash it out with soap every chance she got if I didn't learn to control my potty mouth. Somehow I knew none of that would matter anymore as I took in the stench and the blank stare on my baby brother's face.

The elders say that when someone close to you dies you feel it deep down in your soul. Meanwhile, like a southern thunderstorm true to form, just like that the rain stopped.

However, this time the clouds remained, at least in my heart. I sat in the dark clutching my brother in my tiny bed with nothing but silence all around us.

The beating came to an end. It always does. Like the swift clearing of the rain, I knew she was gone.

Chapter 1

Sidney

Staring out the window of my three story DC waterfront condominium at the summer rain is a good thing as long as I see it as a cleansing process is what my therapist seems to think. You know, god's way of washing away impurities and breathing life back into all living things. I wish it were that simple for me.

You see I've never liked the rain. As a matter of fact I hate it. Instead of breathing life back into my mother I watched it suck it right out of her.

Times like this I sit and stare right through it and back at my own reflection glaring in the glass of my bedroom's bay window. Many say I appear to black out, my eyes showing signs of being removed far from here. I loved that woman. Although I was only ten when she passed, I feel as if I lost a part of me that day. Yes I lost my father to a jail cell barely escaping the notorious death row of an Alabama maximum security prison but to be honest I lost him a long time ago. Despite living in the same household all of my life up until the incident, I never really knew the man anyways. Alcohol was his family and us his enemy.

Do you know I have not seen him once since that day? I hear he is suffering badly from prostate cancer. It runs in our family. I probably should do like the good book says and practice forgiveness. Besides, god has been good to me blessing me with three higher degrees and a career in civil engineering working for the federal government.

Characterized as an overachiever, this thing called forgiveness was the one task I could not accomplish. Besides, if I ever wanted to really forgive him, watching my Aunt Vivi whose now contorted face once a splitting image of my mother's, sit in a nursing facility in a permanent wheelchair, with her tongue hanging out of her mouth, her once beautiful hair matted and strewn about her head, unable to speak a word or utter a sound is the image forever imprinted in my head. It is the image that ceases the idea of forgiveness dead in its track. Like my poor mother…

Ring! Ring! Ring! The sound of my cell phone ringing slowly faded in, interrupting my thoughts.

"Hello. Ms Davis speaking," I said.

"Heyyyy birthday girl, why do you always answer your phone so professionally? Isn't that what caller ID is for?" questioned my best friend of 20 plus years Ms. Nina Simone Anderson. Her name has a nice ring thanks to her mother who absolutely loved the singer and took pride in having her entire catalog.

We met my first day of middle school when my brother and I were sent to live with my Aunt Jennifer and her husband Roy in Washington, DC shortly after my mother's burial which ironically fell on my 11th birthday. A few years later they transferred my aunt Vivi to a facility not far away in neighboring Maryland.

Entering the school house, I remember thinking that I would just fade in with the other new faces from various neighborhoods on the first day of middle school. That plan was quickly abandoned as I ran through the hallway, my penny loafers making music on the floor, with my tin lunch box in hand, and my head down trying to escape the kids who were whispering and making fun of my clothing.

"Go back to your farm," I heard one boy say.

"Did you hear the accent on that hillbilly?" another one asked.

The tears ran down my face and I barely looked up until I ran into a rather tall girl in a fresh pair of British Knights, stone washed jeans, and the coolest Michael Jackson tee, the one with the dancing feet.

"Umm I'm sorry." I said gathering my things which had fell out of my lunch box at her feet.

"No problem," she said bending down to help me. "Are those ugly boys bothering you," she asked standing to her feet now with her hands on her hips.

Before I could reply, she marched right over and punched one and kneed the other right in his privates. She then walked off but not without giving me the thumbs up and yelling over her shoulders "That's Ms. Hillbilly to you yuck mouth and cousin it." To that, all of the kids in the hallway proceeded to laugh and point at the two boys who ran off in pain. Although she was a cool 8th grader, two grades above me at the time, we have been the best of friends ever since.

"Did you hear me girl? I was just calling to check on you. I know you hate the rain but I'm here to be your little ray of sunshine honey," Nina interrupted my thoughts once again.

"My very own Nina Simone," I replied half heartedly.

"Oh cheer up girl. I got just the thing you need. We still on for the party tonight? A girl got to get her freak on to weather this storm," she replied.

"Indeed," I agreed before continuing. "Have you spoken to Jade? You know she has been at an art convention all week in Seattle? I spoke to her briefly yesterday evening but her flight was supposed to touch down at BWI this morning," I said before Nina could give me blow by blow details of what and whom she planned to get into tonight. Trust me, I'm by no means a goody goody but I just wasn't up for the details this rainy morning. With my mom and Aunt Vivi fresh on my mind and my birthday weekend/burial anniversary looming in the air, I just wasn't up for it.

"Girl no, you know Jade be in her high class zone sometimes. She'll hit us before tonight though. You know mamacita can't miss a night of pure bliss to save her life," Nina replied jokingly.

Jade was the newest member of our clique having recently joined our girlfriend circle three years prior. An art buyer for her own gallery also located in Georgetown, Jade was a 36 year old 5'7" caramel coated bombshell with exotic slanted eyes and a perfect size six frame. Conservative in her everyday environment with business suits accessorized by wired rims and her long jet black hair that she wore with neat soft curls that made Remy #1 pack divas envious, Jade had a soft demeanor that greatly clashed with my girl Nina's outgoing personality and style.

However, like Nina and I, while strictly professional during business hours, Jade embraced her freaky side at night. Besides the fact that we were all single professional women with no children, the parties were something we all had in common.

"Girl, you are so crazy. I am going to tell her you called her a freak," I laughed.

"Seven days a week," she replied and hung up in classic Nina style.

Chapter 2

Nina

"Oooh fuck me baby…fuck me bitch!" she screamed in pure ecstasy as I punished that pussy from the back with my deadly strap on Sally as I like to call her.

It was the day of the party but I was getting an early start with this pretty femme I'd picked up at Pink Cashmere a local gay club in Adam's Morgan the night before.

I had just got off the phone with Sidney and after making sure she was ok with the storm that was brewing in the early Saturday sky, that happened to also mark the burial of her mother, and clouded her birthday joy each year, I figured I would go for round two with this sexy 5'4" chocolate goddess with ass for days. I have always been an ass girl if I must say so myself. Besides, my long legs and tits have always been my glory and I love the feeling of getting them sucked. However, there is nothing like riding the big soft ass of a pretty femme as my 36 double D's brush against her crack.

"Ooooooh," she moaned as she bit the pillow in an attempt to muffle the sounds of the pleasure my secret tool was giving her.

As the owner of Red Door an exclusive upscale Adult Toy and

Boutique in Georgetown, I had no shortage of tools. Strap on Sally was just one of many in my arsenal to get the job done, male or female. Oh yes I love a long, black, sometimes international, thick, and wide shaft penetrating my walls too but I will always have a piece of pussy on the side to satisfy my sweet tooth for a certain love juice that only a woman could give. One sip of that juice back in high school and like the Zane book I was "Addicted".

With one swift motion I removed the strap on and replaced it with my mouth while the palm of my left hand stroked this kitten's soft fleshy mound. Now normally I don't eat the ass of a stranger but this one had to be the exception. Slowly I slid my tongue up her crack until it met my destination. With both hands palming her ass now, I slowly parted her cheeks. Around and around my tongue gently circled her asshole while she squirmed and moaned from sheer pleasure. I smacked her ass with both hands and let out a deep moan of my own as it bounced back against my cheek. Turning her over now, it was time to take it to the next level and watch this volcano erupt. Gripping her mouth full breasts with both hands, I commenced to grinding her clit with mines while I sucked on her bottom lip being careful not to allow her to break free of my riding grip. Slow deep moans of pure bliss escaped her lips as she meagerly fought to free her body from my 5'9" frame. When her breathing became shallow and her moans short, I knew she was on the verge of sexual eruption. Immediately I released my grip and moved down south to slowly then frantically lick her swelled clit causing her legs to embrace my head in a locking motion.

"Oooh baby I'm about to cum," she stuttered then shook.

"Tell me where lil mama," I seductively replied coming up briefly for air.

"All over your wet mouth baby," she replied.

With that I decided to put her down for the count. I inserted my right pointer finger into her throbbing wet walls and with a come hither motion I beckoned her G-spot. Slightly covering her clit with my mouth, I slowly licked matching the pace of my inserted finger with that of my tongue. As the soft moans escaped and grew louder with each stroke I sped up the pace. I had no

12

time to concern myself with my flawless short cropped mane as she gripped the sides of my head frantically to brace herself for the inevitable.

"I'm cumin!" she screamed "I'm cummmin!" she yelled again as her body stiffened and jerked hysterically.

That top shelf ass began rising up and down on my sheets to meet my face. With that I removed my finger and gripped both cheeks beneath her, slowing my tongue to a near halt. As she struggled to catch her breath, I smiled smearing her cum all around my lips then licking each of my fingers to emphasize just how tasty her fruit was to me. I then winked and rose up from that sweet spot between her legs and planted a solid kiss on her juicy lips.

Rolling over to my spot I lay on my side and watched her drift off to sleep. In a few hours she would be a distant dream. This was just an appetizer, a prelude to what I had in store for tonight.

Chapter 3

Jade

The hustle and bustle of the airport was as routine to me as my daily 6 a.m. run in Rock Creek Park. With a career as an art buyer for my own gallery, it has become a second home for me. Besides, BWI was minor compared to some of the airports I deal with routinely such as LAX and Chicago's O'Hare.

Besides, nothing could break the feeling of euphoria that I was feeling as a result of the successful business trip to Seattle and the commitment from the hottest up and coming urban painter Jamal Wright, to give me exclusive rights to display and sell his work in my Georgetown gallery. Of course his evident attraction to me didn't hurt the deal but in this business I have long taken that as a part of the game to be used to my advantage to subtly get what I want.

"Your exotic beauty and conservative manner rings mystery to me," he stated during our business meeting, a casual one over coffee and pastries at a local shop in one of Seattle's trendy districts. I absolutely could not leave the city without indulging in Seattle's best. I always heard the coffee was absolutely amazing and since

I try to gain a piece of the culture no matter what city I am in, I obliged.

"Why thank you Mr. Wright but the real mystery is behind your inspiration to create such great work," I replied in an effort to bring the conversation back to the business at hand.

Men love rejection I thought. It's all about the chase. Besides that, my mother taught me it was never proper for a lady to blatantly flirt with a man so playing hard to get was my forte.

To that he smirked and eyed me responding in a smooth baritone voice, "inspiration comes in many forms and that in itself is a mystery."

"Then it's up to us to uncover the mystery that is inspiration," I slyly responded.

Twenty minutes later I was walking out of the shop with a signed contract in hand.

Walking through the airport now, I was on a cloud when it hit me that today was my girl Sidney's birthday. Usually on top of such important things, I realized jet lag must be the culprit. While pulling out my blackberry to speed dial Sid while waiting on my baggage, I made a mental note to call my local florist afterward.

"Hello? Ms. Davis speaking," Sidney answered.

"Happy Birthday girl!" I greeted. "You are now officially a young old head with a few years in your 30's under your belt my sister," I continued.

"I know," she sighed.

"What is wrong sis?" I asked.

At that moment I happened to look up and notice the rain pouring down outside and instantly I knew. In wake of her mother's death, Sidney never did like the rain nor truly felt like celebrating her birthdays. This was something Nina made sure I was well aware of early in our friendship.

"Oh nothing, I'm good. How was your trip?" She asked changing the subject.

"I sealed the....." I immediately lost my train of thought at the site that was now before me.

Approximately 6'3" with dark chocolate skin, bald head, a full close cut beard, wearing a fitted tee, nicely fitted jeans, with Gucci sandals that adorned the most perfect set of feet I had ever seen on a man, leaned before me to pick up his bag from the turnstile.

"Pardon me maam," he simply stated flashing me a smile that could have easily headlined any toothpaste ad I had ever seen. Despite his casually classy gear, had I not been in my right mind I would have sworn he walked right off the pages of one of the many fashion magazines scattered throughout the terminals. He was simply gorgeous.

"Jade are you there?" Sidney asked.

"Oh yes I am here. I thought I saw a client" I lied, smoothing my pencil skirt with my free hand, shifting my weight to my left pump as I slightly turned to sneak a peek at the cocoa Adonis as he walked away and out the door toward the cab stand.

"So where was I?" I continued.

"You were saying something about sealing something," Sidney stated.

"Oh yes girl, I finalized the contract with Jamal Wright," I exclaimed with a touch of pride.

"I am so proud of you mamacita, we must celebrate," she replied excitedly.

Mamacita is what the girls called me because of what they call my exotic flavor. It started a few years back when we went to our first party together after meeting at the grand opening for my gallery, where Nina was looking for erotic yet tasteful art for her toy boutique Red Door which was a few blocks down from my gallery. I don't know what it was but we cliqued and our appetites for unconventional sexual eruption sealed the deal.

At that particular party, after a few drinks to loosen up I was wildly riding this Latin buck and started speaking in Spanish as I succumbed to multiple orgasms. I didn't know I still had it in me but having parents who were well cultured and invested in private Spanish lessons among others during my young life had a way of embedding the language with fluency forever in my brain.

"Mamacita I knew you looked exotic for a reason, you little freak," Nina had said as she smirked and began touching herself

17

from watching my orgasmic session.

That was the same night we engaged in our own little secret before deciding that friendship was best given her tight bond with Sidney and not wanting anything that could potentially break up this newfound sisterhood. It is a decision I am happy we made because I love them both.

In the airport today, the sight of that gorgeous man took me back to that place and made me wonder if he were worth saddling or just another handsome exterior package with a lump of coal inside.

"Celebrate we will just as soon as we finish wearing out the birthday girl with the festivities lined up for tonight" I replied to Sidney now rushing to greet my driver to get back to the city for a brief meeting with my staff at the gallery to fine tune the details of our latest victory.

All of this had to be done before I could go home to unwind with an expensive bottle of my favorite red wine and get ready for tonight.

Chapter 4
Sidney

Relaxing in my spa tub while sipping on a glass of wine was just the therapy I needed after a long day to set the mood for this evening's plans.

Standing in the full length mirror now after oiling my flawless caramel skin toned body, compliments of my mother, with my favorite vanilla scent, I checked out my 5'5" frame pivoting from side to side to see how the black lace bra and thong set accentuated my curves. Ranging from a size six to an eight, I had to work extra hard in the gym to maintain an ideal weight and size.

I partly contribute it to my country upbringing that carried over into my life in DC as Aunt Jennifer never gave up her soul roots in the kitchen. Furthermore, she believed in waste not want not and would not allow myself or my brother to leave the table without finishing our supper. I often found myself eating for two as he was a very picky eater and would sit at the table pouting and on the verge of tears most nights until I saved him by scoffing down his meal when Aunt Jennifer wasn't looking. As an adult, I made a commitment to change my eating habits and work just as hard at my health and body image as I did my studies.

Looking at myself now, I thought the hefty price tag I had shelled out for a spring trainer paid off big time as I looked at the definition in my thighs and arms approvingly. Picking up the paddle brush from my dresser, I began unwrapping and brushing my layered shoulder length sandy brown hair until every strand fell in its desired place. The color was compliments of my father and greatly contrasted the jet black tone of my mother and aunt Vivi.

On my king sized canopy bed I had laid the outfit I chose to pack and change into later. Beside it lay the inconspicuous outfit that I chose to dress in for now. Pulling up a pair of light denim Seven jeans, I walked over to my walk-in closet as I pulled a black matching designer tee over my head and reached for the perfect pair of black Prada pumps. I completed the outfit by walking over to my vanity where I had placed a Tiffany necklace and charm bracelet set on the table top.

Taking one more glimpse in the mirror, "it's your birthday, you can do this. It's only one time a year," I mouthed as I snatched my overnight bag, keys, and black leather Prada bag before flicking the light switch and heading out the door.

Once in my convertible Benz, I let the top down and listened to Janet's "Enjoy" as I pulled out of my parking space. The slightly cool summer's night air brought me added comfort as I hurried to meet my girls. The night was young but what was in store was sure to take the edge off. I hoped!

Chapter 5

Nina

Sitting in the metro parking lot where we met each month around this time and piled into my Range Rover, I was happy to be the first on the scene. This was the one time each month I was sure to be on time with tonight being no exception.

It was exactly 10 p.m. and I needed a minute to just relax after the repeated rounds with the chocolate goddess from earlier. What was supposed to be round two and no more turned into the loss of my entire morning as I dozed off losing track of time.

Thankfully my favorite employee and close friend Brandon could always be counted on to open the store up on time while I recovered from my Friday night romps. I made it a habit to put business before pleasure but from time to time temptation let me rely on my favorite Queen to save a hoe.

"Bitch, you better be glad I don't have a man because when I get one your ass is grass," he shot at me just out of earshot of a nearby customer with his hands on his hips as I strolled in well after 1 p.m. earlier.

"Awww baby I can always count on you to get that beauty sleep and be fierce for mama," I said with a wink while walking to my office in the back of the store.

We went through this all the time but there was a reason I gave Brandon a pair of keys to my store and ensured he was always scheduled off on Friday nights and early on Saturday mornings. I truly trusted and adored him for being so strong despite a troubled background filled with incest at the hands of his great uncle and parents who disowned him after he came out of the closet in high school. I bonded with him as a little brother as I had Sidney as a little sister and protected him no matter what.

Sitting in the car now, I was awakened by a light tapping on my window. I silently cursed myself for dozing off in a dark parking lot as I let Jade in.

"What's up Nina Simone?" she asked kissing me on the cheek as she jumped in the passenger seat.

"Not too much lady," I sleepily replied.

For the next 10 minutes we made small talk, which seemed awkward at times when Sidney was not around, until she showed up last as usual bumping an old Janet track. I watched as she cruised into a nearby parking space and let the top up on her beamer before getting out and sliding into the backseat of my Range.

"Hey ladies" she sang as she dropped her bag and made herself comfortable.

"Hey birthday girl" Jade and I replied in unison. I could tell by the look on Jade's face that she was just as happy as I was that Sidney appeared to be in a good mood.

The ride to the party was light and cheery as we caught up on everything from Jade's new art deal to our latest flings. The topic always went to men with the girls and I because the fact of the matter was that it was hard to find a good man who wasn't on the DL, had no criminal record, a good career, no baby mama drama, and loved black women in the DMV.

According to Sidney we need to look at ourselves to determine why we keep attracting what we do but I say screw that theory. Men need to just be men and until they man up, I'll be happy loving Jane.

Pulling up to the two story home in an upper middle class suburban neighborhood in Maryland, we all hopped out and grabbed our overnight bags. Jade was the first to the door and knocked lightly until a beautiful dark skinned woman, with a coke bottle shape that would put Foxy Brown to shame, came to the door dressed in a white teddy with matching lace thigh high stockings and a white silk robe. I recognized her as Ms. Chantal our host for the evening.

We had been to a few of her gatherings in the past and I had sampled her goods personally a few times before. She stayed dripping wet, could lick a clit, and deep throat the largest cock in no time flat all while taking another up the ass and yet another in her sweet vaginal walls without hesitation. She was without a doubt the reigning queen of orgies.

"Hi ladies come on in," she greeted as we entered the foyer. To our right was her husband, a tall, slim, dark skinned man we only knew as Knight, collecting the proceeds for the evening.

"That would be $10 or a bottle of premium liquor for single ladies" he said as we walked up. "You are looking edible already" he continued licking his lips as we smiled and paid our cover fee.

Immediately all eyes were on us as we walked in the family room where bodies were huddled in corners, sitting on couches, engulfed in side conversations, and sipping on mixed cocktails. All were dressed down for the occasion and to their most intimate comfort level. Ladies were dressed in chemises, teddies, and some in matching bra and g-string sets. On the other hand, some guys wore lounge pants while others wore boxers and white tees with a few bold enough to go shirtless to show off their rock solid six pack abs. I even saw one male who obviously was one of the few preselected single men who were allowed entrance, sporting whitey tighties. That's what I call confidence, I thought as he winked at us as we made our way through the crowd. We casually greeted regulars as we proceeded to the stairs at the back of the room to head up to one of the spare bedrooms to change.

"Ladies did you see what I saw?" Sidney asked in an excited tone as soon as we were in the room.

23

Immediately Jade and I glanced at each other before throwing a shocked expression at Sidney. Normally she lay low and let the prospects approach her, taking her sweet time to come out of her shell, but tonight she appeared to be in lioness mode and on the hunt.

"Who?" I finally asked breaking the silence.

"Girl don't look at me like I'm crazy. The fine, tall cup of tea, in the red boxers, and no shirt hanging out at the bottom of the stairs!" she replied with just as much enthusiasm.

I immediately knew to whom she was referring. I crossed my arms and shook my head saying "let me see you go for what you know then girl. Ride that fire engine ma," while twirling my hips and grinding the air before breaking out in laughter.

Jade immediately put her finger to her mouth and playfully tapped me saying "Shhh he might hear us."

To this I replied "We're all here for the same thing right?" We all stared back and forth at one another before breaking out in a whispered laughter. We then gathered our belongings and headed back downstairs to put away our bags, now filled with the clothing we arrived in.

Jade had changed into a semi conservative yet short light pink chemise, with matching garter on her left leg, and a pair of light pink pumps. She knew how to tastefully show off the most beautiful set of legs I had ever seen on a woman with little effort. I wore my signature red to match the colors of my business. You never know when a networking opportunity may arise so I had to represent in my red lace teddy with matching garter belt, red sheer thigh highs, and fire red pumps. However, the shock of the evening came again in the form of Sidney who wore a black v-cut teddy, with a low v-cut back, and thong behind. To top it off she had on a black garter belt, with matching fishnet thigh highs, and a pair of black and silver pointy toed four inch pumps.

I watched as she sashayed her perfectly round apple bottom down the stairs without a care in the world. Why she hides all of that I have no clue but tonight was going to be different. This was something I was already sure of.

Mingling in the common areas now, we were in our accustomed zone of chatting with regulars and scoping out fresh meat for the night. In the corner I saw Sidney now engulfed in what appeared to be a humorous conversation with the gentleman she had referred to earlier. Jade and I remained together speaking to a couple who we learned were new implants to the area after relocating for the husband's job as an IT analyst for a major firm.

A few appetizers and martinis later we finally heard the call for everyone to assemble in the great room for the reading of the rules. From the crowd Chantal emerged with a microphone.

"Good evening everyone and a special meow to the ladies looking so tasty tonight" she stated in her low pitched and most seductive voice. The crowd gave their own good evening replies in unison while some raised their glasses. To this she gave an approving head nod and scanned the room to get a final collective view of tonight's attendees.

"Many of you have been with us awhile but we do have some newbies in the house so it is important that we go over the rules so we can move on with the festivities," Chantal stated then continued. "Rule number one is no means no. This applies to both ladies and gentlemen. If someone is not interested in your advances, kindly move on. If you are pressured by someone who you have turned down, feel free to go to one of our staff persons who will gladly escort them out," she said before continuing.

"Staff please raise your hands." To this about five hands went up to indicate they were staff members. Dressed down to their intimate comfort level in the same manner as the guests, the only indicator of their status was a chain hanging around their neck that consisted of a single key and name badge that barred their erotic name. Chantal acknowledged them by nodding her head and moved on.

"We have several themed rooms for your tantric pleasure. On the basement level we have a series of poles, swings, and a projector that will feed x-rated videos. No one is admitted on this level with clothing. This area is not for the voyeuristic but playground participants only. Sex is restricted to those areas only and absolutely

25

no sex is allowed in the common areas such as the kitchen, restrooms, and great room. As your invitation indicated no street wear is allowed at this point. Upon entering, all attendees must dress down for the occasion to their most intimate comfort level. Condoms are located at the entrance of each room and the restrooms are fully stocked with toiletries that you will need to freshen up. If you need anything please locate a staff member and they will be happy to assist you. Please do not flush condoms or sanitary wipes down the toilet but instead place them in the waste baskets for proper disposal. Furthermore, if you are here with a person who is not involved in the lifestyle and as a result is uncomfortable, stay with that person at all times to be sure they are ok or just please do us all a favor and go home. Others sense that discomfort and are hindered from enjoying themselves. A few minutes before 3 a.m. a warning will be made that the doors will be locked for the evening for those wishing to spend the night. For those who would like to leave, please make sure you do so by 3:15a.m. as the doors will be locked and the alarm set promptly at that time. Last but not least have fun and do enjoy. It's not Halloween but I see a few tricks in need of a treat. Ha ha ha. I know that was corny but let's get this party started. Enjoy!"

With that the crowd dispersed to locate new prospects or take up the offers of those they scoped out earlier during the meet and greet. Across the hall I caught a glimpse of Sidney retreating to the basement with the sexy man in the red shorts from earlier. Jade and I glanced at each other knowing what time it was if she were going downstairs this early on. This was out of character for her but hey it's her birthday and she deserved to release some tension.

"Well girl I'm going to go see what is going on upstairs. I saw a female trio depart in that direction and shoot I'm in a voyeuristic mood this evening," Jade said eyeing the stairs. "Would you like to come?" she continued.

"No I've had enough female only company," I replied spotting the new couple from earlier headed toward the stairs. "But on second thought…."

I decided I could use some dick after that breakfast buffet from this morning so I took that as my cue to retire upstairs as well.

Chapter 6

Sidney

My girlfriends would squeal with delight if they knew the magnitude of my deep throat. Head game is what the few from my past would call it and it's something many would not expect me, a conservative government engineer, to have. Yet here I lay in this dark basement illuminated only by the soft black lights that shined above my head, licking his shaft with slow calculation and suddenly deep throating the longest blackest dick I had ever seen. Keeping a steady rhythm was especially challenging while engulfed by neighboring arms and legs as orgasm after orgasm could be seen and heard by those around us.

Although distracting at times to say the least, this environment could serve as the backdrop to the greatest orgasm one could have.

As I now circled the hood with my tongue he moaned in pure pleasure as he curled his toes. I watched as he grabbed the hand of a neighboring female when I started sucking his balls one by one and placed them both in my mouth without use of either hand. Sucking then letting them go, I repeated this routine once more before slowly following the undercarriage back to his hood where

I suckled ever so slightly at first and worked myself up until I took one inch more of his manhood into my mouth, and then another, and another before swooping down and swallowing the whole shaft. Then I replaced each inch from the bottom up with a hand motion that caused his body to jerk and his mouth to fly open.

"You're the best baby," is all he could manage to speak.

"Is that right?" I briefly paused to ask.

"Damn baby yes!" he nearly shouted getting the attention of those who had finished their orgasmic session and started gathering now to watch the action that was us.

Moments earlier we chatted briefly in the common area upstairs, where I learned he went by the name KC but those who experienced his sex referred to him as "Superman." I was interested to see if he lived up to that name and jumped on the opportunity surprisingly enough with no hesitation. It was my birthday and it was time that I enjoyed it for once or at least try.

Catching a steady rhythm that increased with each moan, I was now bobbing my head up and down on his thick long cock like it was my last supper. Circling his hood now slowly with my tongue, I was careful not to let a drop of his pre-cum go to waste. It was sweet, a sure sign that he was eating right and that his body in fact was not a façade.

Growing aware of the crowd now gathering to watch my deep throat action, I began feeling like a porn star giving the performance of my life as I positioned my body atop his chiseled frame and began rubbing his shaft between my breasts now upright with swollen areolas that throbbed in anticipation of being pleasured. As his dick met my chin I took an inch of his manhood in my awaiting mouth. When he was on the brink of explosion, he suddenly grabbed me and in one effortless motion flipped me to a position underneath him.

"You want this dick baby?" he asked while sliding a magnum onto his fully erect member.

"Yes," I panted in response.

"Give it to her," I heard a female voice say in the background. To this he entered me with a careful thrust forward, simultaneously releasing a slow gasp "Awww" with his eyes rolled up and his head tilted backward. "Nice and tight" he said as he began stroking my kitty at a steady pace. As he quickened his stroke, my head fell back and my voice got caught in my throat by the thickness of his manhood which now completely filled my walls. Now pumping at a rapid pace, I just knew his dick would come through my head at any moment or at the least I would sacrifice an ovary. However, the pleasure was so intense I could not utter a single word of protest. Pushing my legs further back and leaning in now while taking my breast into his warm juicy mouth, Superman began riding my pussy like a stallion at a winner take all race.

Now releasing an unrecognizable sound of pleasure repeatedly, I was more than happy when someone grabbed my legs and held them spread eagle for me. Staring at his gorgeous brown face, my eyes wandered to his six pack abs which were now flexing and glistening with a small film of perspiration. Just when I thought I could take no more, he flipped me over in one smooth motion and entered me from behind without missing a stroke. Doggy style had always been my favorite position, so I gripped the sheets and steadied myself for the ride.

I did not notice when the light skinned female slid into the empty space in front of my face and began rubbing her clit to the show with one hand and palming my face with the other. Never being one that was into women, I was surprised when my reflexes took over, my mouth opened, and I began sucking her fingers one at a time. "You sexy mother fucker you" she said seductively while continuing to rub her clit with her free hand. She then began inserting her fingers in her vaginal walls and fucking herself to Superman's rhythm while letting out the sexiest moan I had ever heard.

"Oh yeahhhhh" he moaned in response as he placed the palm of his left hand on the curve of my back and rubbed her leg with the right.

She began gyrating her hips until her pussy lips came within inches of my mouth which was filled with her fingers and my own moan that was forever on repeat. The crowd watched in eager anticipation as she removed her digits from my mouth and began softly caressing then cupping my breast with her now free hand. She then removed her other hand from her vaginal walls and licked her own sweetness letting out a soft moan. The smell was intoxicating and for the first time, I was turned on by the essence of another woman.

With each ram from behind, I came closer and closer to her flower. Opening my eyes briefly, I was stunned to see her large almond shaped hazel eyes staring into my eyes with a deep yearning. She then licked her lips and bit her bottom lip while beckoning me with her index finger. Without hesitation, I opened my mouth and covered her pink flesh with my hot mouth, sucking the nectar of the sweetest fruit.

Never being with a woman before, I closed my eyes and imagined how I liked my pussy pleasured. In soft circular up and down motions I licked her slowly then with a faster pace to keep up with the thrusts Superman was giving me from behind as he filled my space perfectly. Soft moans escaped her lips until her song was in sync with our rhythm. With both hands atop my head, she began fucking my mouth with urgency as she fought to keep up with the punishment that was taking place within my vaginal walls.

When it appeared she was nearing the peak of orgasm, she freed herself from my grasp and turned over in the doggy style position and I resumed eating her from behind as she found her own cock to suck. Just like that our threesome had become a foursome.

Nearing the peak of explosion now as I watched her ass jiggle in front of me, I licked her swollen clit, sucked on her pussy lips, and grabbed her ass to brace myself for the inevitable. As my walls began contracting around KC's huge shaft, I felt my whole body shutter as I removed my wet mouth from her flower and let out an indescribable sound of ecstasy. Moments later, I felt Superman's whole body tense before he pulled out, removed the condom, and spilled his seed all over my ass with a simultaneous "Awwwwww!" Next he softly kissed the small of my back and simply said "Happy Birthday" before we collapsed into a heap where we lay exhausted from our session.

Watching Ms. Hazel eyes mount her cock now, I fought to keep my eyes open and watch her pussy lips slide up and down that thick pole before surprisingly contemplating joining them for my own round two. Besides the night was young and it was my day. From the looks of things, a memorable one filled with firsts it would be.

Chapter 7

Jade

"Breaking news, authorities are on the gruesome scene of a condo in a trendy neighborhood of Adams Morgan where a couple was found dead in their home late Sunday evening after a friend went by to check on them after they missed a planned event in their honor, apparent victims of a homicide" anchor woman Leanne Height reported as I tied the laces on my running shoes. *"The names of the victims are being withheld pending notification of the family. We will bring you the latest as this breaking news becomes available."*

Another senseless murder in the city, I thought as I stretched in preparation for my daily 6 a.m. run in Rock Creek Park. Running was therapy for me and was a ritual that not only kept my body in tip top shape but gave me time to think and enjoy the scenery.

From the time I was a little girl, I always enjoyed the great outdoors. Growing up an only child in an upper middle class family in the suburbs of New Jersey, my parents afforded me the luxuries of every private lesson imaginable. They wanted me to be cultured they explained.

However, besides the periodic trips my dad would allow me to tag along with him to the city to purchase art for his Manhattan gallery, the most joyous times of my childhood came in the form of the family camping trips we went on every summer in the Shenandoah Mountains. Although he was raised in the city, my father was a country boy at heart, something he said he picked up from his father who was from the south and died when he was a teenager from complications of the flu. He would often tell me stories about their outdoor adventures and how growing up he often longed for the day that he had his own child to share the things he learned. After marrying his high school sweetheart and many failed attempts at conceiving, I came along.

Although he denies it, I often wonder if he wished he had a male child. Despite being shy at times outside of the home, I was a tom boy until my early 20's when my body finally filled out from its boyish stick figure frame. Given that fact, I'm sure I was as close to boy as he could ask during my youth.

Smiling now, I grabbed my keys and ran out the door to make my daily 5k run making a mental note to call my parents before the day was over. Running through the park now, I had my Iphone playlist set to Michael Jackson. He is the king of pop and will forever be I thought as I watched the men and women of the city clutching their briefcases and almost running to make their commute to work. The people in this city are always in a rush, I thought as I ran along. By my second mile, I was in a zone and they had all but become a distant memory as I further entered the park and followed the trail inhabited now by runners and bikers only.

At the end of my run, I felt refreshed as I walked into my neighborhood Starbucks for my daily frappachino. It was counterproductive but was definitely my guilty pleasure. Engulfed in my own thoughts as I entered the local coffee shop, I nearly knocked him down as he raised his drink to keep from spilling it all over me instead of just my arm.

"I am so sor...." I started when the words became stuck in my mouth. Standing before me was the familiar chocolate frame from the airport the other day.

"It's quite alright" he interjected before I had time to save face.

"I should be the one apologizing. I wasn't watching where I was going," he said before flashing me the brightest smile.

Veneers or clearly a model for the crest ad, I thought to myself. Briefly I imagined what his lips would look like wrapped around my pleasure spot. They were juicy and suckable like that model Tyson. In fact, with his bald head, full lips, and thick eyebrows he favored him but plus a tall stature and minus the gap.

"I should buy you another drink," I firmly stated walking through the door as he offered me a napkin and started dabbing at my arm. The subtle brushing of his skin against mines sent an electrical current straight through my body that caused me to jump.

"I'm sorry" he stated, a worried look replacing that once bright smile. "That was a bit forward of me," he continued.

"Oh no it's the adrenaline, I'm just coming down from my run," I replied while instantly becoming nervous about my sweaty appearance.

"Oh ok," he replied as an expression of relief and that bright smile spread across his face once again.

As he held the door for me while we reentered the coffee shop to reorder our drinks, I noticed his scent was intoxicating. I couldn't help but stare at his lips as he ordered a grande iced Frappachino. Being a gentleman, he insisted upon paying despite my objections.

"How about you make it up to me by joining me for a bit," he stated as he held his palm up toward a table.

Sitting across the table from one another in the corner of the store now, we chatted about ourselves and what we did for a living. I learned his name was Devine and he was a personal trainer who owned a gym in the city. He was born and raised in Washington, DC leaving only to attend college. I filled him in on the gallery and life growing up in New Jersey to my new life in DC. He listened attentively as he stared in my eyes with the darkest most gorgeous eyes imaginable. Glancing at my watch, I realized an hour had gone by and I needed to rush home, shower, get dressed, and head to the gallery.

"I'm sorry to cut this short but I must run" I stated as I stood and gathered my belongings.

Reaching out to shake his hand now as he stood, I was surprised when he leaned in and gave me a hug instead. I almost melted in his arms but gained my composure instead and removed myself from his embrace straightening out my running clothes simultaneously.

"Please take my card," he offered sincerely as he reached into his back pocket and handed me a card.

"Thank you. Unfortunately under the circumstances I do not have one on me," I replied as I looked the card over briefly already wondering what he would taste like as intoxicating as his scent was.

"I understand, we did literally run into one another" he replied jokingly and then flashed that brilliant smile again before continuing "but give me a call. I would very much like to continue this conversation over dinner."

"It would be my pleasure." I responded nonchalantly although my heart was racing.

He responded by smiling and walking me to the door. I waved as he watched me walk away before he turned and headed in the opposite direction.

Sex thoughts were on my mind but something about this one gave me that added touch of difference. He gave me butterflies.

Chapter 8

King

"Davis you get a phone call."

Those words were all too familiar I thought as I rose from the bench in the community cell of the county jail in Upper Marlboro, MD. A few hours prior, I was too drunk to know where I was and how I ended up there along with two of my homeboys Pete and Mike.

Apparently we were charged with disorderly conduct and disturbing the peace outside of a local pool hall. Damn I guess it could be worst being as though this wasn't even my hood I thought as I reached for the phone and prepared to call Sidney.

"Big sis is going to kick my ass if I keep this shit up," I muttered aloud as I dialed her home phone praying she was there although I knew she planned to take the day off to relax after her birthday weekend.

"You have a collect call from...." the recording started and ended with my recorded voice "King". After the standard spill of about 30 seconds, I heard Sidney's voice simply state "what did you get yourself into this time?" as more of a statement than a question.

"Hello to you too big sis," I answered.

"Don't hello me boy," she replied in a tone that implied she was more than slightly annoyed by my call.

"How much and where should I pick you up," she continued clearly disappointed.

After going over the details, two hours later I was walking out of the county jail where big sis was waiting as usual. She has always come through for me since we were kids and I was thankful for that.

Hopping into the front seat of her beamer I leaned over and kissed her cheek before simply stating "I love you Sid." She just nodded and turned the volume up on her favorite Janet Jackson cut before peeling off.

I wished I could tell her this would be the last time she had to bail me out but no use making promises I know I can't keep. One day I'll make her proud, I thought.

About 30 minutes later, we pulled up to her condo. Before she could lecture me I spoke up "Ay yo Sid thanks a million sis for helping me out but I need to make a run to go check on my paintings at the studio."

Despite getting into trouble constantly, and maintaining a permanent residence with Sid, I managed to keep a small studio uptown where I retreated to paint and think when life got out of whack.

"Cool, but don't think you are off the hook Kenny," she replied. Sidney was the only one I let get away with calling me by my government.

To that I kissed her cheek again and headed toward the subway. I knew she was still standing there watching, but I kept it moving without a glance back. How the hell could I face the guilt when I didn't even know what happened.

But anyways, I was actually born Kenneth Raynard Davis but I gave myself the nickname "King" when I started running the streets at the tender age of 11, when I was barely in middle school. That is when I decided I was a king and thus the ruler of my own destiny.

Around that same time, I discovered my love of art after entering a painting called "Pain" into a local art competition at a fine arts center that a teacher had begged me to check out. I won first place easily. Mr. Jackson saw something in me I didn't even think was a big deal and to this day I still don't get the hype. To me, painting is just an outlet, a way for me to express my feelings on paper. No matter what, it will always be my first love but love doesn't pay the bills and I refuse to depend on my sister this late in the game. She's doing her thing and I'm proud but a man has to make his own way out here.

Sidney often got on my case about getting with her friend Jade to display my work in her gallery. They call my work a gift or some shit like that. But I aint ready nor do I know if I ever will be ready to share it with some boogie peeps who only want to criticize a nigga anyways. Jade told me once that those boogie people pay big money for art and drool at new talent, saying I was different but this is one part of me that aint for sale. I'll make my way the best way I know how for now. Maybe one day I'll be down for critique from DC's boogie society but not today. Besides, I suspect they'll see a tall nigga with dreads and think I'm only good for tagging some street corner or neighborhood building for a few crumbs they call a living.

Coming out of the metro in SE now, I headed for the studio to hash out this image that came to me and smoke a jay alone. At that moment my phone vibrated. Looking at the caller ID I saw it was Pete. That nigga could wait.

Later on he would be telling me how we got in this mess and we'd probably be headed to doing some new shit that would land us in the same boat in no time.

For now I'd release my demons through my craft and maybe some ass from this chick whose number I pulled out of my pocket as I reached for my phone. I had no clue how it got there or who she was. However, the DMV does have the baddest chicks in the land so I'll take a chance. I wonder what this one was about.

Chapter 9

Devine

Sitting in my office at the gym now, I daydreamed about the beautiful creature that called herself Jade while twirling a pen around in my hand. I wondered for a second if she remembered our first encounter at BWI. I had not forgotten and could not help but wonder if it were destiny or just pure chance that we ran into each other this morning at the coffee shop.

In my profession, I meet beautiful women all the time that use personal training as a means to get close to me but somehow this one was different. She was classy yet confident and had this air of mystery that drew me in. Even with the sweat pouring from her, she was perfect. No make-up hid her features. She had natural exotic beauty unlike many women who would go as far as wearing make-up to the gym.

I smiled to myself now as I watched one walk by while giving me a wink through the glass that separated my office from the gym. That detail baffled me every time. Mya was her name and I fucked her a few times in the past after she made repeated advances toward me during our private sessions, and to this day I had never seen her

43

without make-up.

She was of German descent and spoke with the edgiest of accents mixing her native language with English from time to time. She wanted more and made that fact clear to me but despite her education and flawless physique there was something that was plastic about her and didn't fit into my idea of a mate even if it were purely physical. Her being married didn't help the situation much either.

At 37, I had years of playboy behind me and had been wondering lately if it were time to retire the game and settle down. So far though, I had found it hard to get to know someone with my busy schedule and the high bar I had set. When I saw Jade in the coffee shop today, I knew I had to take my chances and see if she were worth the risk.

The child of a famous city councilman, I was impressed by the fact that she appeared to have no clue who I was and seemed to genuinely be interested in me during our chat. This was hard to come by in a city this small.

Usually women were attracted to the fact that my father was city councilman Joseph Childs and most wanted to screw me for just that reason alone. Others were looking for a meal ticket or trying to beat some biological clock they set. Women never ceased to amaze me in the sexual arena though. They wanted to assert their independence and use a man for sex just as much as we were accused of doing the same. Until recently, that worked for me.

Lately, I've found myself wanting more. I wonder if it were really me or a result of my father's nagging. He managed to always work himself into even the most minor details in my life.

Ring! Ring! My thoughts were interrupted by the ringing of my office line. "Devine Fitness, Devine Childs speaking," I answered in a professional tone.

"Well I see it's not hard to figure out where to find my oldest offspring and not have my calls screened," replied a familiar voice.

"Hey pops," I said looking down at my cell phone now which I realized was on vibrate with six missed calls three of which were from the councilman.

"My bad, I must have forgotten to turn my ringer back on this morning" I continued.

"Ok son, I was calling to remind you of the gala coming up next weekend to raise funds for the new youth center I am unveiling in ward eight this fall." That was an area of DC that had its challenges but was still considered home to me.

"You may bring a date you know," he stated with emphasis on the term "date". You would think men lived by that same biological clock theory if you spent any amount of time with my father.

"I know dad, I have the perfect person in mind" I lied. However, a part of me imagined stepping out on the red carpet with Jade Alexander. I must be getting soft I thought attributing that fact to getting her last name and remembering it that quickly.

"Great I'll see you then. Right now I'm late for a meeting," the councilman responded a little too eagerly for my taste. However, I was happy it pulled his reigns for now.

"Ok later pops" I responded and quickly hung up the receiver before he could come up with some other reminder of my single status and his disapproval.

I was the oldest of three children 2 boys and the youngest a girl. My brother was three years younger than me at 34 and my sister was a mere 21. She was their "oops" baby is what they often said joking about the fact that my mother was well into her forties when she was conceived.

From the time I was young, my father pushed his expectations on all facets of my life while my mother sat in the background nodding her head at his every command. I loved my mother but sometimes I wished she voiced her own opinion more often. She was a stay at home mother who took on the traditional role of caregiver. She was the best cook in the city in my opinion and with my father gone allot of the time, she tried her best to make sure we had the structure of a normal family. She had a soft demeanor and a warm soul. She would often encourage me to live my dreams but never asserted her beliefs in the presence of my father.

Naturally, when I became old enough to make my own decisions I rebelled. I thank him for pushing me in football the sport I loved because as the star quarter back, it got me a full scholarship to practically any college of my choice. Besides, my love of the game couldn't be swayed by even him. While I did follow my father's commands and attended an IV League school, during my sophomore year I changed my major from political science to business. At my father's persistence I managed to narrowly miss the pros by ignoring the scout's numerous offers of fortune and fame, and continuing on in school. My second love of fitness inspired me to open my own business during my senior year after suffering a major injury that put me out of the game for good. Despite graduating with honors and the promise of employment by major firms as well as my father's continued push for me to run for office and join the political world, I continued to do my own thing and thus here I am today.

Staring out my office window at the people moving about their day, I wondered if she would call and if so would it be practical to ask her on such an exquisite date this early in the game.

With a pile of new member information stacked on my desk, I decided to push the thought from my mind for now and focus on getting some work done. The week had just begun and it promised to be a long one.

Although I had no plans as of yet, the weekend was already on my mind. Despite trying to push her out of my mind, I couldn't help but hope it included the company of a certain Ms. Alexander.

Chapter 10

Sidney

"TGIF!" I said to a passing coworker after gathering my belongings from my office and heading toward the elevator in a hurry to catch the metro.

The weekend was finally here and tonight the girls and I were planning to have dinner before heading to a sexy all white birthday event in the city. Judging by my clock, I had approximately two hours to get home, get dressed, and meet the girls at La' Vie a little French restaurant in NW for dinner.

Typically, a bit of a procrastinator when it comes to preparation, I was happy that I actually took the time to pack my bag for the event while watching my favorite program The First 48 last night.

Despite making it to the restaurant with five minutes to spare, I was the last as usual. Pulling my seat out, Jade kissed my cheek as I took my place next to her and across from Nina at our usual corner booth that provided a scenic view of the trendy district and its inhabitants as they went about their business.

"What's up chick?" Nina greeted as I lay the napkin across my lap and gave our favorite waiter, a cute guy by the name of Pierre, my drink order after he placed a bread basket on the table.

"What did I miss?" I asked as he walked away in the direction of the kitchen.

"We were just catching up on the week's events" Nina replied. "This chick snagged a man and is holding out on calling a nigga" she continued nodding her head in Jade's direction.

"I don't want him to think I am desperate. Under normal circumstances I would give him my number to call me," Jade said in her own defense.

"But you didn't and it has been a week bitch," Nina said jokingly.

"It was just Monday" Jade replied matter of factly.

Watching this back and forth charade for another few minutes in amazement, I decided to intervene when it looked as if Nina had Jade backed in a corner, but not before noticing that the conversation did not once turn sexual. It was not very often that one of us would display genuine interest in a man so I knew this guy must be special.

"Mamacita, bottom line is from the looks of it you are interested but if you don't step up, you may miss your opportunity lady" I stated. "We have been through this and you know what you want so why not give it a shot and do things a little differently this time."

Seeing she was still not convinced I continued "Perhaps the fact that you did not have a card as you stated earlier was a sign."

To this she sighed and replied "Well I guess so. I'll give him a call after we get through this weekend"

"Speaking of…." Nina interjected. "Are y'all ready? My friend Marcel is the planner and I hear he is going all out to make this unlike the regular events. I'm talking black card style. No expenses spared in a lavish hotel downtown. So you know what that means, money in the bank" she exclaimed with a look of joy.

If I did not know better I would think she was a newbie and this was a candy store. "Is that right?" I asked.

I had some information about the event but due to my busy week filled with a concrete deadline on a government contract, I did not have time to get the particulars from Nina who had the contact on this specific event. From the sounds of things and her excitement, I had a feeling it was exclusive as well.

"Seems that way, and with business growing at the gallery, I may even let my guard down and entertain a future client given the caliber of the guest list," Jade responded to my inquiry.

"Hell it's always the prime time to mix business with pleasure in my line of work," Nina said still grinning from ear to ear.

After another two hours of dining and chatting I glanced at my watch and realized we had struck the ten o'clock hour which meant it was time to satisfy our check and move on to our next destination, a five star hotel in downtown Washington, DC.

Despite, being anxious about what was in store, my mind could not help but wander on the ride over as I sat in the passenger seat of Nina's Range Rover. I had not spoken to my brother since I had picked him up Monday from the county jail, nor did his room appear as if he had been there. The latter was not uncommon as he kept clothing and essentials at his small studio and often disappeared for days at a time, but he always called me to check in. Taking notice of my mood, Nina stepped in to offer a simple "He'll turn up, he always done"

To this I gave a half hearted smile. My best friend knew me like a book. In an attempt to lighten the mood, I turned the volume up and we all threw our hands up in unison as the words "welcome to my sex room" filled the SUV. The night was still young and we were on the prowl.

Chapter 11

King

Kim was her name and it turned out she was a sucker for a nigga with artistic talents among others if a dude got to pump himself up for these broads.

After getting a long overdue shower and putting in some work at my studio earlier in the week, I decided to try my hand with the number I had pulled out of my pocket from that wild night when Pete, Mike, and I got caught out there in PG County. She remembered me although I hadn't a clue who she was or what she looked like for that matter.

Nevertheless, I conversated with her while digging for clues the entire time. To her, we were getting to know each other. After 30 minutes and still no clue I decided to step this up a notch and ask her to meet up with me later at a local spoken word café for a drink. If my nigga Pete could hear the invite he would most definitely clown me on the spot.

I had known Pete since we were kids and in fact he was one of the first I met on the playground when we moved to DC when I was just six. He kicked dirt on my new school shoes and tried to punk me in front of our other classmates. Feeling a sudden urge even at that tender age to lay down the law, I kicked his ass on the spot. After getting a few days of hard feelings out of the way, we were tight ever since.

Mike was Pete's wild younger cousin who was in college but still wanted to hang with the fellas. I think his sheltered life in Montgomery County gave him a warped view of the streets and he felt he had something to prove. I didn't get it and often told him to stick to the books. Pete on the other hand, encouraged him and real talk if I did not know better I would think he was a little jealous as their mothers were sisters and often compared notes.

But anyways back to the ladies. Pete always said I put in too much work with these broads to get some ass. A nigga hates to admit it but deep down I enjoy the chase as well as the company outside of the bedroom. One day I'll settle down but in the meantime, I have to grind and pussy is still on the agenda. So I invited her to the spot and she came through.

After a few drinks, and learning we had met at the pool hall we got kicked out of, I was shocked when she made the first move and invited me back to her place. This was Monday night and here it is Friday. With the exception of heading out to the studio a few times to finish my piece, I've been here ever since.

This bitch had some lethal ass, and until this very moment it had not dawned on me that I had not checked in with big sis. My phone had long been dead and I never went by the crib to pick up the charger.

Sitting on the edge of the bed now, I picked up her home phone and dialed Sid. "Hello" she answered on the first ring.

"Sid it's me" I replied sheepishly now feeling guilty because I knew she had to be worried. The only time I took this much time to check in was when I was locked up.

"Boy where the heck have you been? I have been worried sick," she stated in her best attempt at an annoyed tone. My sister was worried but she was a sucker for me and I could tell she was just happy to hear my voice.

"Sis, my bad I have been busy all week. I decided to follow

some leads Jade gave me on my work," I said feeling bad that I was lying but I could not let her know "ass" was the only reason I neglected to check in.

"Well ok me and the girls are pulling up to this birthday event so you better call me first thing in the morning. I'll talk to you later" She responded with what I thought I detected as a sigh of relief.

"Later" I simply stated and hung up.

As I flung my legs back into bed, I felt a hand creep up my thigh and grab my manhood. This chick is an animal I thought as I felt my manhood spring to life at that slight gesture. Stroking it through my boxers now, I licked my lips and placed my hands behind my head as Kim climbed on top of me fingering one of my locs.

"You ready for another round?" she said in a sleepy yet seductive tone.

Although I was hardly what people would call dark-skinned, her light skin greatly contrasted against mines. She was what we called red-bone. She was so light in fact her milky skin resembled that of a white woman's. With a short Halle Berry cut, dark piercing eyes, and juicy nude colored lips she had a sexy natural look. With a small waist, curvy hips, and a fat ass, she had the body of a stripper. She was tall with a set of long lean legs that ran for days.

How did I forget this one? I thought as she began slow grinding on my dick with her head cocked back and her hands on my chest. I laid back and enjoyed the faces she made for a moment before taking over. Removing my hands from behind my head now I reached up and covered each of her perky breasts, circling each nipple with my thumb while admiring them both.

"Mmmm" she moaned.

Sitting in the upright position now I began kissing her neck as she wrapped her long legs around my waist, straddled me, and continued slow winding her hips to an imaginary reggae beat as I continued to play with her titties. With my dick now at full attention, I'm sure it felt like a rock on her ass and I was ready to cut the bullshit and introduce her to some shit I had not done the entire week I was there. At this moment my dick throbbed at the thought of what her juicy ass felt like.

Lightly pushing her onto her back, I climbed on top of her now and began grinding being careful not to enter her walls. With her eyes closed she moaned in pleasure and her legs spread further and further apart in anticipation of what I was about to do to that pussy. I had different plans though and it was time to test the water.

With one hand still firm on her breast, I used the other to flip her over on her stomach. Leaning close to her ear while grinding my dick against her ass, I inhaled a deep whiff of her floral essence before suddenly leaning back on my knees and pulling her ass in close to me.

Reaching for a magnum on the nightstand, I quickly removed the wrapper and slid the condom on my 10 inch rod. Her ass in the doggy position was picture perfect. I kissed each cheek and slid my tongue down her crack before slowly easing the tip of my dick in her asshole. Surprisingly she lifted her ass slightly higher in the air, then grabbed, and spread both of her cheeks apart in anticipation of letting me all the way in. Inch by inch I tested the waters slowly as she let out a long and exaggerated sigh as each inch filled her anal walls which tightened to the conformity of my massive member. As I filled her more and more her sighs and moans gained an octave until she was singing soprano as I slowly pumped her asshole. As it loosened on my dick, I increased the force behind my pump until I was punishing that ass at a steady pace. She bit down on the pillow and moaned in pure ecstasy as I rode her ass like it was her pussy showing no mercy as she began cursing in the sexiest high pitch.

"You're fucking my ass," she screamed. "You're fu fu fucking my my my my ass nigga!" she stuttered as she allowed her stomach to fall flat onto the mattress.

To this I grabbed her by her petite waist and pulled that ass back into my stroke. Putting my hands on her shoulders now I braced myself as I fucked her asshole without an ounce of lube. By now she was making her own juices and they flowed as well as her pussy.

Turning her head now, her mouth opened to suck on my

fingers. I placed my fingers in her mouth and continued stroking her ass. Nowhere near out of gas but on the verge of explosion, I slowed down as her ass rose and fell to meet my dick on its own without my assistance. I watched as she bounced up and down to her own rhythm and to my amazement. There were not many that could take all of me and especially not in the ass. Her pussy juice drenched my balls as my dick filled her anal canal. I listened as she came and her body jerked no longer able to control the multiple orgasms it had built up.

Grabbing her by the waist now, I pulled out only briefly to flip her on her back and resume my stroke in her pussy which was throbbing and overflowing with her juices. Upon entering her, it immediately tightened around my dick.

"Mmmm you're so big baby," she said in that seductive tone as she grabbed my ass and pulled all of me into her walls.

I began my signature slow grind before pulling halfway out slowly and reentering with a commanding force until my rhythm had her weak in anticipation. I watched as she came again and again.

When I thought she could no longer take it, I pushed her legs back as far as I could behind her head and stuck two fingers up her ass as I punished her pussy with my dick. She screamed and said something I could not make out. On the edge of explosion myself now, I pulled my dick out and grabbed the condom in one swift motion before cumming all over her face and into her waiting mouth.

"Arghhhhh" I managed to growl before she swallowed and began smearing my remains all over her pretty face as I collapsed in a spent heap beside her. All of my energy was now gone.

Tonight I must sleep I thought and it would be the best sleep I had in months.

Chapter 12

Nina

Pulling up to the fabulous five star grand hotel, we all jumped out with our overnight designer bags as I tossed my keys to the valet who could not help but stare at my mile long legs and grin before hopping into the driver's seat of my freshly waxed black on tan Range Rover.

I was accustomed to that unsubtle gesture from males and females alike and often wore short skirts to show them off. Tonight was no exception.

At that moment, I wondered if he knew what type of event this was. Giving a wink and kiss in his direction I walked around the back of my vehicle to meet my girls on the curb as we prepared to make our red carpet entrance.

Looking up at the 20 story Cartwright hotel I could not help but marvel at the idea that the host of this event, internationally known architect, designer, and owner of this lovely structure, Jonathon Cartwright must have serious cash to shut down his entire operation for the night.

Furthermore, it had not slipped my mind that celebrity party planner and my close friend Marcel Bennett, who happened to be our ticket in to this exclusive event tonight, was the man responsible for planning this event. It was no secret that his events carried a hefty price tag because of his reputation among Hollywood's elite.

Starting out as an event planner who organized local political events, his big break came when he was referred by a senator to one of his famous actor friends who found himself in the city at the last minute without a planner for a major charity event he had scheduled in Washington, DC. Inquiring minds really wanted to know if the fact that he was sleeping with the "happily married" senator helped fuel that referral. It didn't matter though because his fabulous ideas would always overshadow that theory in my book.

I grabbed my girls by the hand and although we floated on a red carpet, we knew there would be no cameras flashing tonight. There were only two hefty men standing stoic outside of the main entrance each holding one hand behind their back.

Those in this lifestyle went to great lengths to ensure their discretion and privacy would not be compromised by their participation in freak nasty sex. Today, those measures would be stepped up for this private invite only event as the crowd was sure to be the elite and prestigious members of society who definitely had a reputation to protect. Everyone who was somebody scandal worthy would be in attendance tonight.

As we entered the atrium we were greeted by two beautiful women, one white and the other of some Asian descent. Each was holding a bouquet of single white roses. Both were dressed in simple yet exquisite short black sleeveless dresses with matching black pumps. Each had on a simple black cap that resembled that of a bellhop with their hair pulled neatly back into a bun. I could not help but notice that both had on a striking shade of red lipstick with a silver chain that adorned their neck with a single letter C as a charm in a sparkling diamond cut. Impressive, I thought.

After giving us each a single white rose, we followed as they led us through a grand corridor and down one flight on an escalator that led to the hotel's pampering spa which adorned the title Hidden Oasis above its magnificent arched entry way. We walked through a set of frosty glass doors with huge brass handles into what was the locker area. The room was huge for a changing area and was filled with white roses to match the color scheme for the night. Some were in vases while others were meticulously arranged and scattered throughout the room with a trail of rose petals leading from the doorway to the changing area.

The shorter of the ladies with the blond hair and huge blue eyes, instructed us to completely disrobe and change into a white robe and matching slippers that we could find in either of the melon colored lockers that had not had their keys removed thus far. We were told that this was in preparation for a full body massage prior to changing into our wardrobe for the evening. Exchanging looks, the girls and I were clearly impressed at this unexpected added bonus.

As instructed, after disrobing we rang the tiny bell to be escorted to our individual spa treatment rooms which were dimly lit with the air lightly scented from aromatherapy and the sound of light waterfalls playing in the background.

I sat back and enjoyed my full body massage by a sexy Latino massage therapist who went by the name of Carlos. He was extremely handsome standing at what I calculated to be at least six feet with olive colored skin, jet black shoulder length hair, high cheek bones, a single dimple, and rock hard oiled up six pack abs that I could not miss as he only wore all white pants with no shirt and white flip flops. Even his toes look perfect, I thought as I imagined sucking each one under a cabana.

Refusing to allow him to cover an inch of my body with the provided sheets, I seductively switched positions when following his instructions. I moaned and gyrated my hips as he worked the kinks out of every inch of my body. With my eyes closed, I imagined what it would feel like to have his Latino manhood inside of my throbbing and now perfectly wet walls.

Thirty minutes and four orgasms later, which I did not hide, I stood up to exit and relieve Carlos from the torture of watching me masturbate to his massage technique as I continuously exploded right before his eyes. I licked my lips as I looked at the massive bulge that filled his pants before turning and sashaying out of the room, without my robe, toward the shower area to meet my girls without a glance back. He would no doubt be beating his meat furiously before his next session I thought as I went to prepare for the big fun I knew lie ahead.

After taking a shower and playing with my pussy to relieve a final nut that built up instantly at the site of the bulge in Carlos pants, I met my girls in the changing room. Each looked as if they had a similar experience but the need to confirm was non-existent among my girls and me.

While getting dressed, we made small talk about the anticipated upcoming festivities.

"Judging by the service thus far, I think this will shape up to be quite the time" Jade stated as she sat in the changing area oiling her body next to a two piece all white number that broke the mold of her semi conservative chemise style.

"I know! That massage was definitely a great prelude" Sidney giggled as she pulled up the straps to her pearl white chemise that dipped and cut right above her ass in the back. She was getting more and more comfortable with her sex appeal lately, I couldn't help but think.

"I don't know about you two but I plan to be a high class hoe tonight," I laughed as I smoothed the belly area of my high cut white teddy that accentuated my mile long legs which I left bare for the occasion.

To this we all laughed and finished dressing before giving each other a nod of approval and preparing to exit the double glass doors from which we entered. Waiting for us on the other side were the two ladies who had escorted us earlier. They led us back up the flight of stairs and to the lobby where we caught an elevator to the roof top floor. When the doors opened, our eyes brightened at the site before us.

Walking off the elevator, the ladies nodded and said "enjoy your night" in unison before retreating back to the elevator.

"Impressive," Sidney stated. To that we nodded.

We were standing in a grand room with huge crystal chandeliers and large vases filled with white roses. Huge columns extended from the floor to the ceiling. Straight ahead we could see where it, the ceiling, ended and the night sky began. Tucked in each corner of the room was a grand bar set up with half naked bartenders wearing little more than white Armani boxer briefs and white bow ties. The ladies wore white laced thongs and white neckties that did little to hide their full perky breasts.

We walked in the direction of the outdoor bar where we were instantly greeted by waitresses who wore one piece white leotards, white pumps, and a single string of white pearls in their hair. They offered us drinks and hors d 'oeuvres which we gladly accepted.

"I can get used to this," Jade stated as she sipped on a glass of Moet.

"I concur" I stated as we all clinked are glasses in a toast.

"Let's see what's on the rooftop," Sidney said pointing in the direction where the ceiling ended and the night sky began.

When we reached that point there were three stairs that led to the rooftop which had a massive Olympic sized swimming pool and Jacuzzi filled with naked bodies. Instead of chairs, the pool was surrounded by queen sized beds with white canopies and white silk bedding. Couples were sitting on the beds engaged in conversation clearly anticipating the coming announcements so they could partake in more engaging activities.

Admiring the view with my girls, at that very moment I was tapped on the shoulder. Turning to see who was ready to size me up for a later rendezvous, I almost passed out at the sight before me. Standing at about 5'10", average build, caramel colored skin, with beautiful bedroom eyes, and a sexy pair of lips that screamed "suck me" was a serious blast from my past.

"I see you are still as lovely as ever," he stated in his southern baritone slightly licking his lips and giving me the once over in five seconds flat.

His ability to make you feel like he could devour you while maintaining his swag and air of mystery was a characteristic he possessed since we were children. Even I, a self proclaimed diva could melt on contact from that look alone.

Instantly, I was taken back to when we were children growing up in New Orleans before my family relocated to DC and we were forced to carry on summer romances. Only one year older than me, he was my first everything.

At the tender age of 13 he was the first boy to reverse my tomboy ways and make me realize I liked boys. Relentlessly he pursued me as I played hard to get. He was my first kiss and at the age of 15 he took my virginity. Through the pain and despite our ages I somehow knew even back then that he was my soul mate. Each summer I anticipated seeing him and it was not until he left for college and I did so the following year that we lost contact. Even today as I stood frozen in place he gave me butterflies.

"Jay?" I questioned letting out a small sigh realizing now I had been holding my breath. Was this a mirage?

"Yes Nina baby," he replied in that sexy baritone ending with his infamous smile revealing a set of perfect pearly whites. His real name was Jeremiah Carter but he has always gone by Jay.

"Ladies," he continued nodding in the direction of Sidney and Jade who both simultaneously let out a small sigh of their own, apparent victims as well.

"Oh I apologize, these are my girlfriends you remember Sidney and this is Jade" I said gathering my composure and extending my hand in each of their directions as I introduced them. To this he grabbed each of their hands and kissed them.

"My pleasure," he crooned. Both were speechless.

He then turned toward me and gave me a warm hug before kissing both of my cheeks. The smell of his cologne took my breath away once again.

"I am sorry I do not want to be rude so I will leave you ladies to mingle," he directed to us all. "Always a pleasure Nina and ladies it was nice seeing you," he continued addressing us with his hypnotizing set of eyes.

"Ok" we all stated in unison with our mouths slightly left agape as he turned and walk away.

As soon as he was out of earshot Sidney leaned in "Girrrrrllll he looks better than ever."

"Damn where have you been hiding all of that Ms. Nina?" Jade stated wide eyed and pointing in the direction Jay had retreated.

"He's an old friend" I replied nonchalantly but my girls knew me better.

"I would say he's more than that," Sidney replied.

"You have met the one guy that can tame Nina Simone," she continued cutting her eyes at me and turning to look at Jade now giving her a high five.

I just stood there trying not to look stunned as I nursed the drink I forgot was in my hand. I had to get that before I left but somehow I felt like it was more than sex I was after. We had unfinished business judging by the overwhelming feeling that was taking over me.

Chapter 13

Jade

Despite the lavish surroundings and the star treatment the girls and I had been receiving thus far, my mind was wandering to earlier in the week when I met Devine.

After seeing Nina's reaction and her obvious love for Jay, I wondered if I should have called him by now. I was not one to pursue men but under the circumstances I had not given him my number at the coffee house that day after my morning run so I had to make the first move. What would I say? Does he really like me or was he being polite since I did spill my drink all over him?

Standing here watching the couples engaged in conversations in the nearby canopy beds, I couldn't help but daydream about what he would look like in this sexy setting. I made a mental note to call him on Monday before I made my way into the gallery. For now I had to push him out of my mind one way or another and try to enjoy the rest of this evening.

Just then as the girls and I were engaged in small talk after letting Nina, who was obviously blushing and uncontrollably nervous, off the hook my eyes wandered to my ticket out of my own funk for the evening. He winked and tipped his glass in my direction. I did a brief check to see if my girls had noticed and they hadn't so I tipped mines back at the chocolate stranger.

A few minutes passed and Nina scooted to a corner to engage in further conversation with Jay and Sidney asked if I would be ok before making her way to one of the canopies with a guy who looked vaguely similar to Mr. Red Boxers from the party a few weeks back. In this atmosphere one could not always tell if they were crossing paths with familiar faces as they all looked the same when the clock struck 12 and the lights went out.

Standing alone now sipping on a daiquiri, I noticed the chocolate colored gentlemen from across the room whisper to a clean cut light skinned gentleman next to him and proceed to walk in my direction. As he approached I slightly turned to the side to appear as if I did not notice him approaching.

"Excuse me beautiful," he stated in a deep baritone slightly touching my arm with one hand while holding a glass of champagne in the other.

"Hi" was all I managed to reply sheepishly.

He was more gorgeous up close and personal with a huge left dimple that formed as he smiled at me slightly.

"I know this may seem forward and presumptuous even under these circumstances but my friend and I was wondering if you would care to join us? No pressure however, if you'd rather one of us just watch."

He then continued eye balling me with the sexiest set of hazel brown eyes that contrasted with his dark skin. I looked him over from his perfectly caesared hair cut and slightly crooked smile to his perfectly tailored white linen pants and well pedicured toes. I desperately needed some distraction from thinking about Devine and the prolonged phone call that I could not put off any longer so I agreed.

Grabbing me by the hand, he made a slight nodding gesture toward his equally handsome friend and led me to a canopy in the far corner of the room where we could have an audience yet maintain a sense of privacy.

Knowing the DC area was not excluded from the high population of bisexual men I could not say for sure if these two just wanted to tag team me or if there was more. At this point as long as there was protection involved I did not care. I needed to get Devine off of my mind and maybe it would take two beautiful men to do the trick tonight.

However, despite the well put together presentation before me, when compared, neither could spark the interest that had ignited in me from the encounter with Mr. Devine. In fact I imagined his gorgeous face and bald head when Mr. Chocolate began stroking my mane and then stopped to run his fingers across my cheekbone. I imagined him as his fairer friend rubbed my thighs with the softest fingertips and managed to catch a glimpse of his juicy lips as he kissed my knee caps one at a time.

My head fell back as Mr. Chocolate kissed my neck with the softest kisses that trailed down to my shoulders and back. At that very moment I imagined Devine as his fairer friend sent a trail of kisses from my knee caps to my toes stopping only to suck them one by one savoring them with his eyes rolling in the back of his head. I lifted my head to see his manhood rise as he followed that trail back up north to meet my pleasure spot, now dripping wet and swollen with anticipation and desire.

I managed to let out a slight gasp as his lips locked on my fleshy mound before licking it softly in circular motions. I felt my head fall back once more as Mr. Chocolate found my hardened nipples with his soft mouth and began sucking ever so gently while holding my neck steady in the palm of his left hand and my free breast in the palm of his right as he circled the areola with his thumb.

"Mmmmm" I moaned as I imagined Devine's thick juicy lips covering my sweet spot which was now contracting with pleasure as the fair skinned gentleman inserted his pointer and middle fingers into my walls which perfectly gripped them as I avidly practiced my kegel exercises daily. Not once did he come up for air as he finger fucked me while licking my clit with urgency now. Orgasm after orgasm escaped her depths as I squirted my love juice down the back of his throat and he swallowed it eagerly before beckoning

67

her for more.

I couldn't help but think of Devine's perfect Colgate smile as Mr. Chocolate smiled down at me with his somehow perfectly crooked smile and asked me "Do you like it mami?"

"Yes papi" I whispered before he covered my mouth with his own and began French kissing me to the same beat that his friend was circling my clit to as if we were all in sync with our own beat.

Normally I did not kiss strangers but somehow the thought of Devine passionately engaged in this kissing experience with me made me forget the true playground participants that were here.

I did not hesitate when he broke the kiss and his fair skinned friend flipped me over before continuing his feast from the back as my perfectly round ass became the focal point of Mr. Chocolate who was now leaning over my head and planting kisses on each cheek before standing straight up to greet my mouth with his massively thick pleasure rod which was throbbing with anticipation and dripping with pre-cum. The site of it sent my taste buds in a frenzy causing me to stick my tongue out and gather the drop that was forming, before circling its contents around the head of his dick.

"Yesss" he moaned as I licked the bulging vein that had formed on the undercarriage of his shaft while turning my head to the side to take his balls into my mouth one at a time releasing one only to gather the other while closing my left hand around his girth simultaneously.

I did not flinch as I imagined Devine's big hands as Mr. Fair Skin slapped my ass before running a trail from my pussy lips up the crack of my ass from behind. My ass rose to meet the viscous tongue lashing he was administering as he tossed my salad. This deepened the bend in my back and caused me to slightly gape my mouth open as I held onto Mr. Chocolate's manhood bracing myself to keep from succumbing to the immense pleasure he was sending through my body.

Once I got my composure again I filled my mouth with the massive erection that was before me imagining what it would feel like to have Devine's rod fill my awaiting mouth. He held my head, allowing his head to fall back as his knees became weak from my oral pleasure.

I didn't care who was listening as I let out the loudest moan when Mr. Fair Skin entered me from behind and filled my walls with the thickest girth I had felt in a long time causing me to slightly miss a beat as I deep throated Mr. Chocolate. For a moment, I wondered if Devine would enter my tight walls with as much urgency and determination.

He did not miss a stroke as I struggled to catch his now furious beat as I sucked the manhood which was getting harder in my mouth with each passing second. I felt it throb and pulsate to the same beat as my vaginal walls which were gripping the thick pleasure rod of Mr. Fair Skin with the same fury. It was at that moment I recognized the tune that was playing on the speakers that reached the rooftop deck and I imagined Devine riding my pussy to the same strong beat that this sexual tune was provoking.

"Mmmm…Ahhhhh," we moaned in unison as my pussy became wetter and wetter and the two massive penises that filled my spaces became harder and harder with each stroke and suck. I knew the buildup was near its peak as I felt two pair of hands tighten their riding grip on my juicy ass, as well as two on either side of my mangled tresses, and my own spot swell in anticipation of the inevitable release.

At that moment, as if on cue Mr. Chocolate released a mouth full of creamy cum down my throat before falling back on the mattress of the canopy we inhabited, sweat filling his brow. To that I gripped the sheets and steadied myself as my own explosion poured out of my already dripping wet pussy and the words "I'm cumin daddy" escaped my lips in a barely audible gasp. At the same time I imagined Devine's seed filling the magnum sized condom Mr. Fair Skin was filling deep within my walls.

"Argghhh," he yelled as he shook from the final drop before falling back into his own heap on our canopy as my body collapsed simultaneously into Mr. Chocolate's awaiting arms.

He smiled his beautifully crooked smile at me as I giggled nervously preparing myself to come down from the Devine filled fantasy these two evoked in me.

Unfortunately these two did not take my mind off of him but they gave me just the motivation I needed to make good on that promise I made that could not go unfulfilled on Monday.

Chapter 14

Nina

"Breaking news! Police are on the grounds of a Potomac mansion where local celebrity and event planner Marcel Bennett was found dead early this morning, an apparent victim of a homicide. He is best known for the lavish political and celebrity events he planned in the DC area and other major cities throughout the U.S. No word has been given on the exact cause of death or motive. Stay tuned as we continue to provide you with the latest on this tragic situation," anchor man Tony Sims reported as live areal images of Marcel's mansion grounds flashed across my television.

I could not believe my ears as I sat up in bed listening to the breaking news report. Immediately I began sobbing as I watched the police escort the gentleman from the coroner's office as they brought my dear friend out, covered on a gurney, and put him in the back of a white van.

"What's wrong baby?" Jay asked as he sat up in bed rubbing his eyes.

After spending the rest of the weekend making love and spending time together, he decided to extend his stay in the city through today. He planned to catch a flight out early Tuesday morning back to Houston, Texas where he had relocated his business after the storm.

He was an architect and had his own firm. Seeing him at the event brought back memories of our young New Orleans romance and the drive he had even back then. He loved building things as a young teen and was responsible for the first club house he and his friends turned into a teen hang out spot in the bayou.

They made money charging teens in the area an entrance fee and using one of their other homeboys, who was a talented DJ who later went on to be a semi-famous professional DJ in Miami, to spin music and keep the party vibes all the way live.

Thinking about Jay then and seeing him now ignited a passionate fire within me that I did not know still existed. It was obvious we had unresolved business. Never had I felt the type of connection with a lover as I had with Jay and I'm not going to lie, it scared a person like me who was used to being in control of my emotions.

However, I could not deny that having him here now holding me as I learned of this devastating news was something I desperately needed. At this moment, I was happy that he was here and that I had Brandon to cover for me at my boutique both today and tomorrow as I would definitely need some time to digest this information.

This is simply unreal, I thought as Jay and I sat in bed, him holding me with my head in his chest as he rubbed my arms and whispered words of comfort in my ear. Knowing she would be at work and most likely had not heard the news, as she disliked watching the news about as much as she hated the rain, I decided I would call and catch Sidney up later on this evening if the news did not spread like a wildfire before then. If so, I knew she would be calling me.

Ring! Ring! Ring! The sound of my cell phone broke me out of my sobbing frenzy. Looking at the caller id, I saw that it was Sidney.

"Hey girl" I managed in a solemn tone.

"I am so sorry Nina" she replied just as solemnly picking up on my tone. "I came up from the dungeon as soon as I could to call you. You know that government building has no reception in the basement where I work," she continued.

"It's so unreal. Who would do this to him?" I began sobbing again as Jay pulled me closer.

My phone beeped and I saw it was Jade. After conferencing her in and spending a few more minutes venting to my girls, we agreed that they would meet Jay and I for dinner at La'Vie this evening before hanging up.

Staring in his eyes now, I was surprised at how easy it was to open up to him after all this time. It was easy and came as natural as the air I breathe. There was no denying it, he was quickly tearing down the walls I had built around my heart for so long. He was my first and only love. Being with him now was like he never left my life.

We had spent time catching up and he did not flinch when I told him my deepest secrets including the fact that I was bisexual and had been involved in the lifestyle for many years now. He let me know that he was not in the lifestyle, but had been invited to the Cartwright event by a close business partner. However, he did not judge me and although he didn't believe it was something he could ever get into with the one he loved, he was quite intrigued by the freedom from inhibitions that he witnessed that night at the party.

Laying me down now, he climbed on top of me and stroked my cheek with his right hand as he continued to stare deep into my eyes and let me know he was right here for me and everything would be ok. My heart fluttered as he ran his fingers through my short cropped mane never breaking eye connection. I rested my chin in the palm of his hand as he ran a trail with his fingertips from my hair, along my jaw line, and down to my breasts before replacing them with his awaiting mouth. Not before blowing his warm breath across my fully erect nipple in a manner that sent chills down my spine causing me to arch my back.

To this he grabbed my hips and pulled me closer into him entering me with one long exaggerated slow thrust. Immediately my walls conformed to his manhood, a natural fit as I let out a low sigh. For the next hour we made sweet passionate love. Something I had not known in forever.

Chapter 15

Devine

I have to stop screwing this chick I thought to myself as Mya walked by my office with an exaggerated twist of her hips as she waved at me through the glass which separated my office from the gym.

After a long week filled with small catastrophe after catastrophe at the gym I had been looking forward to the weekend when I would shorten my hours at my business and take some time for myself.

I still had not heard from Ms. Jade Alexander so I took that as a disappointing sign that she was not as into me as I initially thought or she had a man. Women of her caliber were rarely truly single.

As I faked a smile and waved back at Mya, I could not help but think about how I had accepted her proposition to meet her at an upscale hotel this past Saturday night. She had said her husband would be out of town and she desperately needed to "talk" to me. I knew what that really meant but decided at the last minute that it would be just the thing I needed to block the constant images of Jade which had began to cloud my mind. After hours of adulterous

75

sex, I snuck out of the bed in the middle of the night and retreated to my oasis.

That night the sex definitely did not do the trick as Jade was all I could think of to keep my nature rising. The minute I was back to reality, I realized Mya just could not do it for me and I couldn't stand to spend the night with her. It just wasn't in the rules regardless of the fact that she did not have to rush home this time. Truth be told, I actually liked it better that way.

Today I wished I could take this weekend back as I watched her sashay down the hall obviously engulfed in her own feeling of victory. I knew the time would come when I would have to let her know there was nothing between us and I would start right now with the physical.

I shook my head and continued working when suddenly my phone started vibrating. I had to remember to turn it back on each Monday. I always made it a habit to turn it off or on vibrate on Sunday evenings so I could have some uninterrupted me time for a few hours since it was rare I could find the time otherwise. I did not recognize the number so I answered in my professional voice.

"Hello, Devine Childs speaking," I said.

"Umm, hello Devine how are you? This is Jade from the coffee shop," she replied in a soft beautiful voice that instantly made my heart flutter.

"I am doing well miss lady from the coffee shop and you?" I responded slyly trying not to sound too excited.

"I can't complain," she answered with a small chuckle. "Another Monday and I still have clients. Yes even in this economy," she laughed seeming to enjoy the ice breaker.

For the next 15 minutes we chatted about small things catching up on the past week while vaguely discussing our uneventful weekends. She apologized for taking so long to call and I eagerly accepted. We chatted as if we were picking up on our conversation from the coffee shop without a pause in between. She remembered details that surprised me about as much as the details I remembered about her. The conversation flowed naturally.

I did not fail to notice how she allowed me to lead and she

gracefully joined in like such the lady. After a few more minutes, she explained that she had to prepare for a meeting with an art dealer in a few hours. I explained that I would very much love to continue our conversation over dinner. She declined stating she had to meet her girlfriends later this evening but would like to take me up on that offer later in the week.

There was no way I was letting her go without getting her contact number and at least starting the ball rolling on dinner plans. I knew of a great spot downtown that had a nice cozy feel and would be perfect for a first date. I asked and she agreed also taking me up on the offer to call her later on tonight. I felt like a man on cloud nine by the time we hung up.

I leaned back in my chair and closed my eyes wondering how I was going to get through the rest of the day. I smiled as I imagined her face and the sweet sound of her voice.

When I opened my eyes, I was unpleasantly surprised to see Mya standing in front of my desk staring back at me with a mischievous grin of her own spread across her face and both hands on her hips. Her make-up sure was flawless for someone coming here to workout I couldn't help but think.

"You must be happy to see me," she said with a smirk. Instantly, I lost my cloud and almost lost my breakfast at the very same moment.

"Mya, I did not hear you come in," I simply stated. "How may I help you?" I continued professionally.

"I wanted to talk to you about the other night. You left before I could serve you breakfast" She said seductively.

"About that, we do need to talk" I replied completely ignoring her attempt at seduction.

I knew the day would come when we had to have this conversation so we might as well make it now I thought as I stood up to close my office door and prepared myself to explain why there could never be an "us," being careful to emphasize her husband for the sake of my business and her sanity.

What a day filled with extreme highs and lows this was becoming already I thought. At least it would end on a high note named Ms Jade Alexander I told myself as I braced myself for the inevitable.

Chapter 16

King

"Damn my nigga it's like that?" My man Pete asked as soon as I answered the line.

"Man what's up?" I replied chuckling.

"I'm just saying yo a nigga been trying to get at you all week but you been laid up ha ha," he said laughing.

"A little something," I replied thinking about the past week and how it got away from me weekend included. She had a nigga bunned up something viscous so I was glad to finally be back in my studio working on my craft.

"I'm here in the studio now, so what's really good?" I continued.

"That's what I was calling you about, Yo hit me with some work you down?" Pete said.

He killed me with the "Yo". He was originally from Baltimore so everybody was "Yo." I knew exactly who he was talking about though and was more than ready as my paper was real low.

"Come scoop me up man I'll be here," I replied.

"My man" he said before hanging up.

With Pete I knew I was working with at least an hour before

he showed up so I decided to finish up my piece before hitting the shower. True to form about an hour and a half later at approximately 11 p.m. Pete came through and we headed uptown to meet with his connect about getting our weight up.

Like I said before a nigga got to eat and although it aint always good money, fast money is exactly what I needed right about now. Besides, my supplies are running low and I aint about to hit baby sis for no ends because she does enough for me. On the other hand, I know she'd do anything to keep me off the streets and would happily oblige but not before giving me the "Jade" lecture on selling my craft. She was always telling me about how Jade would love to make a deal with me. I loved my big sis and sometimes I have to admit the thought was tempting but when I sat and thought about selling out to boogie society that thought was dismissed. In a few days I'd be straight though so I pushed that out of my mind for now.

Pulling up to the spot which wasn't far from my studio in SE, I felt a sickness come over me for some reason. Suddenly I realized I hadn't eaten all day. I made a note to get Pete to drop me by the carryout on the way back to the crib in SW.

"Yo, I'll be right back" Pete stated before getting out of the driver's seat of his late model Impala and making his way to the two story brick building in the projects giving up dap to a few fellas who were on the stoop shooting dice.

The rule was one man and we knew the game well so I sat in the passenger seat watching the scenery which included a group of broads walking by in short shorts with rainbow colored hair. I licked my lips as the short one switched her fat ass from side to side obviously craving the attention and attention she got as the fellas abandoned their game to heckle them. A few minutes later I watched Pete exit the building before climbing back into the driver's seat.

"We're in my nig" he laughed as he gave me dap and prepared to crank up the engine on his Impala when suddenly…

Pop! Pop! Pop! Followed by screams was the last thing I heard as I watched Pete slump in his seat, blood running down his temple.

I recall shaking him violently.

"Pete nigga shit what the fuck?" I said panicking before patting myself down for holes. I didn't feel any pain but next I felt a warm sensation oozing down my neck before my eyes began to blur and my mind began drifting taking me far away from here.

I don't recall anything after that. In fact, the next thing I remember is waking up to small beeps in a hospital room, tubes running from my body, with Sid sitting right by my bed side. I remember her jumping up looking disarrayed before yelling for a nurse. I blinked my eyes hard a few times trying to focus on the contents of the foreign room which looked blurry. I tried to open my mouth to speak but no words would come out and instantly my throat hurt. I realized I had tubes running down it. Damn. I struggled to move around to no avail.

"Hold on baby bro, a nurse will be here shortly," Sid said a look of worry then relief spreading across her face as she watched me attentively running her hands across my forehead.

At that moment two nurses came running followed closely by what looked like Nina and Jade both looking as disarrayed as Sid. I guessed they had all been here awhile. It took few more moments before I realized where I was exactly and what had happened. Instantly I began to panic as I thought about my homie slumped over the steering wheel, sending my monitor in a frenzy as my blood pressure climbed.

"Calm down sweetie, you're all right" the hot petite nurse said as she administered something in my IV.

I shot a look at Sid hoping she could calm my fears but she quickly turned away and into the arms of Nina who watched the nurses work furiously on me. Within a few minutes my monitors were all under control and I was resting again.

Apparently, I had been in a coma for two days a gunshot wound to the neck. My boy Pete had taken one to the head and one to the shoulder. I'd later learn he did not make it but instead died instantly leaving another young child, a girl age six, without a father.

I could relate as that was the age I was when my father killed

81

my mother and I lost both parents that summers night in a country shack in Alabama. Damn.

Chapter 17

Sidney

Why me lord? I thought as I watched my brother in a coma suffering from a gunshot wound to the neck. It had been two days since I received the news and the outlook wasn't looking too good. With him being in a coma nothing could be done at the moment about the bullet still lodged in his neck.

My girls Nina and Jade had been by my side the entire time as well as Jay until he had to catch his flight home on Tuesday. I was happy he and Nina were in love. He brought a side out of her that I was unaccustomed to but it was beautiful. I loved the way he handled her with tender care and looked into her eyes, genuinely concerned about her well being. He was always the perfect gentleman attentively catering to her needs. I hope they do not lose contact again I thought before my mind drifted back to the present situation and my brother laying there showing no signs of life other than the support monitors he was hooked up to with their constant slow beeps.

There was no word on what happened that night, suspects, or concrete motive. The best the detectives could put together at this point was a possible robbery attempt which may be drug related based upon what they found on Pete. They definitely planned to question Kenny if he pulled through.

I watched as the cops who were placed on 24 hr surveillance of his hospital room, due to the nature of the case, switch posts for the evening. At that moment, I was reminded there is a god when baby brother suddenly started stirring.

Instantly, I sprang to action and called for the nurses who came running and began working on him. I have always protected my brother but I felt helpless in this situation as his monitors beeped loudly setting off alarms.

When he suddenly started panicking I knew from the look he gave me that he was anxious to find out about his friend. Unfortunately, Pete did not make it and I could not bear to look him in the eyes and confirm his suspicion. They had been friends for as long as Nina and I.

Growing up together, Kenny and Pete were inseparable. From the time they were small boys playing ball at the park together, to the time they were young men chasing girls, all the way until now when they ran the street together you rarely saw one without the other. Although I complained and often voiced my opinion that Pete was a bad influence on Kenny, I loved him all the same.

Pete was like a second brother to me and it was hard hearing the news but I definitely did not want to lose Kenny too. He is the only family I have besides my girls and I couldn't dare stand the thought of losing him. With Aunt Vivi in a home and the fact that we rarely spoke to Aunt Jennifer and her husband, we sought each other even more for that sense of family.

Growing up, I often thought Aunt Jennifer blamed us for the death of my mother. I know that sounds bad but I think we served as constant reminders to her of our father and the permanent destruction he caused in their lives. So when we became grown we naturally grew apart from her with the exception of occasional phone calls.

Therefore I was surprised when she came to the hospital yesterday so soon after I left the message about Kenny. She took one look at him laying there with wires and tubes running from his body and I thought I saw tears well up in her eyes before she turned her back to me. This was surprising because I could count the number of times I saw her cry which were very few and far in between. Having a reputation as a strong woman, she barely shed a tear even at my mother's funeral. Instead she sat there at the burial with a stone face rubbing Kenny's back as he sobbed and asked why they were putting his mom in the ground.

She had a weak spot for him and would often let him get away with mischievous behavior while being completely strict with me saying that young ladies should not do certain things but boys would always be boys.

Not knowing how serious Kenny's condition was now and fearing the worst, she pulled me aside and had a private conversation with me saying she could not hold on to the information any longer in case he required medical assistance from a relative. The information she divulged caused my own miniature health scare as the nurses rushed to my aid from the small fainting spell it caused.

The man sitting in an Alabama maximum security prison who we knew as our father, turned out to only be my biological father.

My mother Carolyn met and started dating my father Earl when they were in high school. He started abusing her shortly thereafter giving her a black eye the night of their high school homecoming dance during her junior year. This happened to also be the night she found out she was pregnant with me. Despite being urged to terminate the pregnancy by friends and family, she went through with it and had me at the tender age of seventeen. The beatings got progressively worst until she was finally forced to take a stand. She took everyone's advice and left my father one day after he knocked two of her teeth out while she held me in her arms narrowly missing dropping me on the floor.

She hid from my father and had all but given up on love until she met a young handsome local aspiring musician and talented painter by the name of Louis Kenneth Walters. They instantly fell in love and he treated her like the queen that she was showering her with gifts and confessing his love as he sang songs that he wrote especially for her. According to Aunt Jennifer, he would never put his hands on her other than to touch her tenderly and protected her with every ounce of his being. He adored me, tossing me in the air for hours on end and would often give me treats when my mom was not looking much like Aunt Vivi. My brother completed their union making him a proud man.

When Louis found out my mother was pregnant, he passed out cigars to all of his buddies and pushed up a wedding proposal he already had planned according to those closest to him. However, one day after a gig, he and his fellow band mates were struck by a drunk driver. Louis died instantly leaving my mom eight months pregnant and deep in depression.

Not wanting to bring a second child into the world out of wedlock, she went back to my father and married him at a justice of the piece shortly after.

From the time he was born it was clear that my brother was different showing talent in art as early as elementary school.

According to my aunt Jennifer, Earl and my mother would often fight and he would call Kenny a bastard child never voicing this to us but treating him different all the same.

Replaying our life with him and trying to make sense of the startling new revelation as I watched Kenny's nearly lifeless body, I wondered how I would break the news to him if he did pull through. This brought a new wave of stress crashing down upon me.

However, seeing Kenny spring back to life now after laying vacant and showing no signs of life for two days brought me some much needed relief. I knew the recovery would be long and slow but we will get through it, I thought.

Even now as I sit here watching him sleep peacefully, I know this to be true despite what the doctors say. They do not know just yet the extent of his injuries and whether he will walk again but I know my brother and he is a fighter so there is no doubt in my mind that he will do just that and be back to creating his masterpieces in no time. At least now I knew where it came from I thought smiling.

Despite getting in trouble allot, Kenny is a good person and I hope this experience, as unfortunate as it may be, is the wake up call he needs to turn his life around. Lord knows he does not need to become a statistic at the age of 27. Now that god has given him a second chance, I am not having it! He is talented in so many ways he just needs to see it like the rest of us and use his gift for his own betterment.

"Are you ok sweetie?" Nina interrupted my thoughts.

"Yes hun," I replied sighing.

"Is there anything we can get for you, you look flushed?" Jade asked a worried expression on her face.

"I am fine mamacita," I said with a small smile trying to assure myself as much as her. To that, she and Jade came closer and gave me a hug letting me break down and cry for the first time since the incident occurred.

I had become so accustomed to being strong for my brother that I did not realize how much I had been holding inside until that very moment when I knew he would be alright.

Chapter 18

Jade

Cell phone in hand I made a dash to catch the metro train as I wrapped up a call with Devine and finalized plans for our date tonight. It was Friday and what a long week it had been.

Our plans to meet earlier in the week were derailed by numerous incidents and my later than anticipated night at the gallery was almost proving to be another thorn in my side as I sat in the nearest seat catching my breath.

Right after King came out of his coma, Nina hit us with the latest news she had into the death of her friend Marcel Bennett whose funeral was this morning. We all attended the heartbreaking ceremony which is part of the reason I was late getting out of the gallery tonight. The who's who of society all packed The Greater Missionary Baptist Church, which was one of the largest in the city, to pay their final respects and mourn the loss of one of the greatest event planners the city had known.

We were shocked to learn that his death was being connected to a series of deaths that had taken place during the spring and early summer months including that of a young couple who had recently moved to the area. I vaguely remember hearing that story as I prepared for a run one morning a few weeks earlier. The scariest part of the investigation is that it revealed that there was possibly a serial killer and sexual predator on the loose in Washington, DC. Nina had heard firsthand from Marcel's family that top notch investigators were being brought in from all over the country to look into this high profile case.

Shock followed by fear swept my sister circle as we wondered if the lifestyle had anything to do with these recent developments being as though the last time any of us saw him alive was when he chatted with us briefly at the huge Cartwright event he put together last weekend. The event was grander than grand. We quickly dismissed that theory because neither the event nor the underground lifestyle had been mentioned in the media who had swarmed the story, hungry for details into his final days.

As I sat on the train now I tried to get the earlier events out of my head so I could enjoy tonight with Devine. I closed my eyes and imagined his flawless cocoa colored skin, deep dark eyes, succulent lips, beautiful smile, and tall athletic build. This man was picture perfect I thought as I slightly smiled enjoying the picture that had invaded my mind.

Although we did not get to meet earlier in the week he took the time to invite me to a Gala that he was attending tomorrow night. Being as though we had not been on a proper date, I thought I may feel a little uncomfortable about going on such an exquisite date. However, I quickly dismissed that thought when he assured me that we could go as friends and that it would be a great opportunity to network for my gallery. His subtly and the way he put me at ease continued to intrigue me so I obliged.

Even now I put the thought of what I would wear out of my mind as I focused on the mental image of his being that was implanted in my daydream during my ride home.

When the train reached my stop, I hurried off to make it to my condo which was two blocks away. I barely spoke to the bellhop as I breezed through the lobby. He was always so friendly and eager to greet me but tonight I was absorbed in thought as I scurried past him and onto the elevator to my 11th floor luxury condominium.

After entering the key in the lock I was instantly relaxed by the cozy warm environment as I made my way to my master suite and lit my favorite candle before kicking off my pumps and making my way to my walk-in closet which was meticulously organized courtesy of the best in town. Instantly, my eye was drawn to a hot red number which was sexy enough to grab attention yet simple enough for a first date. I rarely wore red but tonight I was feeling on fire from the nice daydream I had on the train and wanted to make a lasting impression without overdoing my look. I pulled it from the closet and lay it on the bed as I made my way to the master bath and began running a hot steamy bubble bath with my favorite vanilla scent before lighting the matching candles that surrounded my spa tab. I loved scented candles. There was something about them that was so relaxing.

Looking at the time, I was happy I had a little time to treat myself to this bath as the nerves began to sink in as it got closer to finally seeing him face to face again and on planned terms. Stepping out of my black pants suit, I placed it in the dry cleaning hamper before wrapping my long mane and stepping into the awaiting bath which felt wonderful.

Thirty minutes later I got out feeling refreshed as I prepared for my date making sure to top it off with my favorite scent and killer red pumps, pinning my hair up for the occasion. I was careful not to be overly sexy by letting it flow down my shoulders. Giving myself the once over I nodded in approval as I quickly switched purses, grabbed my keys, and headed out the door to meet the man of my dreams at a downtown restaurant, anticipation and nerves steady rising.

Chapter 19

Devine

Tucked away in a quiet corner booth, I positioned myself to have a bird's eye view of the main entrance of the dimly lit restaurant as I nursed my water waiting for Ms. Jade Alexander to arrive. A few minutes later, she entered wearing a gorgeous red dress with her hair pinned up in a manner that accentuated her beautiful face. My jaw almost dropped at the site of her beauty.

I watched as she scanned the restaurant looking in the direction I had provided a few minutes earlier via text message. I raised my hand to signal to her and she gave a bright smile and headed in my direction before saying a few words to the hostess who was attempting to assist her most likely with looking up her reservation or finding her party.

I stood as she approached the table and leaned in to hug her slightly lingering from the intoxicating scent that was emitting from her glowing skin. I extended my hand in the direction of her seat.

"Ladies first," I said before watching her take her seat and following suit.

Sitting across from each other now, there was an awkward silence as I tried to form my words still marveling in her beauty. I thought I sensed nerves coming from her as well as she blushed and smiled at me. I said a silent prayer of relief when the waitress came up and introduced herself asking if she could start us off with an appetizer and something to drink before running down the specials for the day. I ordered a bottle of white wine after asking Jade her preference. She then smiled and asked for a few more minutes to go over the menu. I tried not to stare as I glanced over my own menu to steal a peek or two at her radiance. I already knew that I would be having the pan seared salmon and asparagus so I was using this opportunity to take in how gorgeous she truly was. When the waitress returned and poured our glasses we finally began to relax after we toasted and had our first drink.

Once the nerves subsided, we immediately fell into our normal conversation laughing and making small talk about the gala which was scheduled for tomorrow. When the timing felt right, which happened to be over dessert, I gave her the run down on my father explaining who he was and that he was hosting the gala for a cause that was near to him. Judging by her lady-like qualities, independence, and family background, I was almost positive this would not change her image of me or her agenda.

For once, I was not concerned that a woman would see this as a self centered opportunity but instead I actually rather feared she would not want to come any longer for fear of moving too fast in meeting my parents. I was pleasantly surprised when she took this new information and showed no signs of concern or fear of meeting my parents. I felt this may be contributed to the fact that I told her we could go as friends. Perhaps this took the pressure off so I was relieved that we had that conversation earlier.

As dinner neared an end I satisfied the tab and asked her if she would like to go for a walk along the pier of the DC waterfront, not at all eager for this date to end.

She glanced down at her pumps before laughing and saying playfully "Not a chance in these pumps sweetie".

I looked down and could not help but chuckle as well.

"What if I gave you a ride home to change into something more comfortable?" I asked before smiling and continuing, "I'll wait in the car if it puts you at ease" sensing a slight hesitation.

"Sure" she replied. "I would actually love that" she continued smiling as well showing a beautiful set of white teeth.

With that, I extended my hand to help her up and we walked out to meet the valet. On the ride to her home, we talked some more laughing about old school music trivia that she was surprisingly good at. I thought I was the old school champion but she was running a close second.

We had allot in common and I could not get enough of her wit and charm. I was exceptionally turned on by her surprising sense of humor which I found adorable. When she started spitting lyrics from Grand Master Flash, I could not help but bebop as we pulled into the circular entrance of her condo. I watched as she blew me a kiss and exited the car as the bellhop held the door for her.

"I'll be back in two shakes" she giggled as she disappeared inside of the lobby.

I sat back in my seat and smiled at how she was continuing to warm up to me and seemed to be more open than her classy appearance signaled. This woman continues to amaze me, I thought. Hands down, she had it all wrapped in one large pretty bow. I have to admit she had me from the beginning as I knew there was something special about her.

However, I was a little concerned that she may be too independent and not exactly on the market for a relationship after she took so long to call me. However, those thoughts were quickly placed in the back of my mind after she called and we had our first conversation since running into each other at the coffee shop and I didn't plan on looking back. In fact, I was beginning to wonder if she was the one and if I could ever ask for more.

After a long romantic walk along the pier followed by the sweetest kiss good night back at her condo's main entrance, I had to pinch myself to be sure I was not dreaming.

Perhaps my father was right and it was time for me to settle down. One thing was for sure, she had me wide open. At tomorrow's gala, I would walk in proud to have her on my arm for the first of many special nights I hoped.

Chapter 20

Nina

"Mmm hmmm, you have flowers Ms. Thang" Brandon said with his hands on his hips and a quizzing look on his face as I entered my boutique Red Door from grabbing a bite to eat at a local Italian sub shop.

Following behind me, he peeped over my shoulders as I grabbed the card from a beautiful summer arrangement with sprays of lilies as the focal point which was my favorite flower. Besides the fact that I had cut everyone off instantly from my black book of fun, I immediately knew who sent them and I smiled. Jay was one of the few people who knew my love of the flower, I thought as I prepared to open the card.

"Thank you but do you mind girlfriend?" I turned and asked Brandon with my hands now on my hips as well trying my best to look annoyed.

"Excuse me missy, I guess we'll talk later" Brandon said flamboyantly twisting his hand in the air and pivoting on his heels to leave but not before smacking his teeth for added drama.

I shook my head and leaned over to inhale the fresh scent of the gorgeous arrangement before opening the card.

"To my first and last true love, may your smile never fade yours truly and in every sense of the word, Jay," were the words printed on the card.

A new wave of butterflies hit me as I grabbed my cell and dialed his number. What in the world is he doing to me I thought, as I smiled waiting for him to pick up.

"Hello sweetheart," he said in his sexy baritone.

"Thank you for the flowers love, I see you remembered" I replied sitting at my desk now and leaning over to get another whiff of the herbal essence.

"How could I forget a thing about you baby? You are everything to me," he said letting his voice drop another octave emphasizing the word "everything".

This sent chills down my spine and I tried to keep my voice from wavering with emotion as I replied "and you are everything to me, thank you again sweetie I will call you as soon as I leave the boutique."

He chuckled slightly and replied "I look forward to it, enjoy the rest of your day baby."

I smiled and shook my head as I ended the call and tried to gain my composure before facing a million questions from Brandon. I love him but he had to be the nosiest person I knew and with the drama of the past few weeks this was one thing I wanted to enjoy myself.

Jay and I have loved each other from the beginning and as fate would have it we crossed paths again so I knew it had to be destiny.

Besides the recent death of Marcel and the crazy circumstances surrounding the investigation of his death, the past few weeks had been hectic. King had been shot and was now recovering so I had to keep it together for Sid while fighting these hoes and the men from my past who just didn't get the fact that I wasn't down for a romp in the sac with them today or ever again as far as I was concerned. It was hump day and I normally would have a little something lined up to celebrate but not today. I was missing my boo and he was the only thing on my mind.

Shaking my head as I left the confines of my office, I thought about how deep that was for me because I loved sex without the complications but somehow this didn't feel complicated at all.

I tried to busy myself with checking inventory but couldn't help but notice Brandon eyeing me from the side of his eye as he helped a customer with the latest dildo on the market that I was sure she would be punishing her own or somebody else's pussy with later on. She had freak written all over her as she eagerly palmed the hand crafted penis and felt its life like material while anxiously licking her lips. I winked at him and continued working until I spotted Sidney coming in the door dressed in her corporate attire.

My eyebrows rose as I waved to signal her. She never came in much during a work day unless she had important news on her mind that she could not discuss in open spaces such as her office in the basement of her government building, which had zero cellular reception. I watched as she waved at Brandon who started grinning. I swear he is a closet straight guy sometimes the way he gets excited whenever he sees Sidney.

"Hey hon" she said slightly out of breath, as she kissed both of my cheeks.

"Hey babe everything good?" I asked now concerned.

"Does something have to be wrong for me to visit my best friend?" She asked putting her hand on her hip and raising her eyebrows.

"No sweetie, you just came rushing in here all out of breath," I replied chuckling. "You need a midday fix?" I continued pointing at a stash of new sex toys that came in.

"No, I mean yes I could use it but that's not why I'm here silly," Sidney said. "You had lunch yet?" she continued.

"I picked up a sub from the shop down the street," I replied. "Why, do you need to talk because I don't have much going on? Between Brandon and Rachel I have plenty of coverage?" I continued.

"Yes hun that would be great if you can," she said and I thought I caught a hint of worry and anxiousness in her tone.

After grabbing my purse and leaving Brandon in charge, I

headed out with Sidney. We walked along the trendy neighborhood of Georgetown that held my boutique and made a left into a very cozy residential neighborhood before she began talking.

"Nina, there are two reasons I wanted to talk to you," she said sighing. "One, I am very concerned about the news that is breaking. There is talk all over my office about a sexual predator and serial killer being on the loose in our backyard. Have you heard anything new about the investigation into Marcel's death?" she asked a look of worry obviously written on her face.

"No all I have heard is that there are top notch investigators being flown in but they are keeping the details hush" I replied stopping our walk and turning to face her to carry on our conversation.

"Well I know there is a party this weekend but I think we should sit the next few out until they find out what is going on," she said looking me in the eyes.

Secretly, I was happy because I really was not feeling it right now with all that was going on and my rekindled love on the horizon.

"That is fine by me love and judging by the cloud our girl Jade has been floating on named Devine, I don't think she will mind much either," I said chuckling a little trying to lighten the mood.

"I know right, she is trying to keep it on the hush but I know her and she is wide open," Sid said smiling now. "Looks like I'll continue on in Singleville alone," she continued.

"Girl, I'll try this relationship thing but you know I travel that city well," I said laughing out loud.

"You will be just fine," she said hugging me now.

"There was something else you wanted to discuss missy so you are not getting off that easy," I said looking at her with one eyebrow raised.

"Oh yeah well it's not too pressing so I'll hit you up and we'll talk about that later" she said brushing the subject off.

"Are you sure?" I asked with one eyebrow raised, knowing my best friend.

"Yes Nina Simone," she said assuring me that everything was ok.

"Ok, you know I'm here," I said hugging her this time before we started on our journey again. We continued walking and chatting about less heavy stuff for another 15 minutes before heading back to our offices.

I purposely did not bring up King or his shooting incident because I knew it was heavy on her mind and she needed a break from it, if only while she was at work. I love my best friend and no matter what we would get through these trying times together that was for certain.

Walking back in the boutique, I could not escape Brandon's eye so I sucked it up and prepared to tell him all about the love of my life including a few juicy sex details to hold him over if only for a moment.

Chapter 21

King

"In the case of 4 yr old Jeremiah, you are not the father."
Damn these chicks be on some scandalous shit sometimes, I thought as I lay in bed at Sid's condo trying my hardest not to shake my head and send a piercing pain through my body. Maury was a guilty pleasure and now I had plenty of time to watch it as I recovered.

It had been a few weeks since the incident, and I was glad to finally be home from the hospital. According to the doctors I was lucky. The small caliber bullet that entered my neck just missed zone one which was considered the deadliest zone, with zone three right behind it, to injure in your neck as it housed most of the major vascular structures that can cause hemorrhaging, paralysis, and sudden death in many cases. I was lucky because the bullet just missed my jugular vein but caused minor spinal injury, thus the crutches lying by the side of my bed. Despite all that, my prognosis was bright as I had full function of all of my limbs although they were weak and slow to respond. With aggressive physical therapy the doctors were confident that I would be back and fully functioning with limited complications.

I was happy that all bullshit medical jargon aside I would be ok with time but I couldn't help but feel fucked up for my boy Pete who didn't make it. His cousin Mike is taking it bad and I aint gonna lie, talk of revenge has come up between us but the streets is dry on the subject. In a small way I'm glad it's that way for now to give that nigga time to calm down because he has school and a bright future. If he straightens his act up and stops trying to live the thug life on the side he'll be straight.

The word is that our shooting was a robbery attempt gone bad, but if that's the case why didn't the niggas grab our stash and run? Unless they were some lames who got scared, this shit was fucking mind boggling. I could slap myself every time I replay that night because I am normally up on my game and watch my surroundings but I did not see this one coming at all.

Despite being in critical condition at the hospital and now that I was fresh out of the hospital, the police have been on my ass questioning our every move that day. I can't count the number of detectives that have left me their card after hearing the same shit over and over. I don't know shit and I don't remember shit besides being shot. Of course I know the routine though. I have been questioned plenty of times in other cases. They aren't trying to solve our case for real. It's a front to keep the mayor and chief of police front in center as caring representatives of the city who want to solve murders. The reality is this shit will soon turn cold and they will disappear faster than they came.

Besides, I don't have shit to give them and if I did I'm not sure I would because snitching is still a major crime in my hood and street justice seems to send the right signals in my book.

Sitting up in the bed watching Maury now, I wished there was a way that I could lay down without feeling crazy pain despite the meds I was constantly popping these days. Even sitting up was a task when done for long periods of time with sudden movements sending sharp pains through my neck, which was bandaged tightly, and my body.

Just as I was adjusting myself for the hundredth time today, I heard Sid come in. Glancing at the time, I knew she had to have taken an early personal leave this afternoon to be getting in this time of day. I was on the second run of the show which aired again at 2 p.m. and I was barely into the first commercial when I heard her keys.

Coming into my room, she stared at the TV as the program came back on and back at me before laughing out loud. She was obviously amused at my choice of programming.

"Boy, is this how you will be occupying your time?" she asked stopping with her hand on her hip before relaxing and giving another chuckle as I made an attempt to shrug my shoulders and smile.

"How was your day sis?" I asked in a hoarse voice. I still had not recovered the full use of my voice which hurt when I talked.

"It was just fine, don't overwork yourself," she said frowning as she scurried over to my bedside after witnessing me whence.

"I need to get a pad and paper and set it by your bedside so we can communicate the long old fashioned way because I don't need you straining and hurting yourself further" she said. "Matter of fact I'm calling the doctor right now" She continued turning to head out the room.

"Noooo," I managed to moan.

She turned and looked at me as I attempted to give her a pleading yet reassuring look to let her know I was ok and did not need the extra attention.

"Ok but I'm only giving it a few days and I'm voicing my concern Kenny," she said in a defeated tone.

"I know, I know," I said trying to shake off the pain.

"Ok well there is something I want to discuss with you after you get some rest," she said frown lines reappearing on her forehead.

"What's up we can talk now," I said straightening myself up a little more in bed.

"You know I love you little brother, but no you get some rest now and we'll talk later for sure," she continued turning once again to leave the room but not before shaking her head at the TV screen once more.

My sister acts so old sometimes to be so young. Sometimes I think she feels the need to be a mother figure to me since we lost ours. She was always overprotective of me but that went up about ten notches after that tragic day and it showed today as she treated me like a juvenile rather than a grown man who happened to get caught up in some shit.

When she left out and I was convinced I had enough of Maury for the day, I tried resting but my phone would not quit. Kim had been blowing me up since she learned I was being released from the hospital. I had every intention of calling or at least texting her, as she did hold me down while I was in the hospital, but I was unsure what to say to someone who was nothing more than a sex buddy harsh as it sounded. I was shot but I still did not get it twisted. She was a beast in the bed but that was about it. Real talk, things moved too fast between us for me to ever take her serious for real. Besides she didn't seem interested in much more than partying. I know I'm far from the picture of the model man but I know eventually I'll want more and she aint it. That is one thing I was certain of.

After turning my ringer off, I did the same with the TV, before adjusting myself the best I could and closing my eyes for a few. I knew if I became too comfortable the dreams would come but I was in need of some rest and I'd deal with the dreams if it meant some relief from this constant pain.

More and more these days I was beginning to think maybe sis was right. Maybe I should be counting my blessings and concentrating on turning my life around. Maybe I would give Jade that call after all. Art was my life so I might as well start there. What is the worst that could happen? I know my craft is tight and it might as well be my ticket out and from under my sisters wing for once but for now sleep was the number one item on my agenda and I succumbed to it allot faster than I thought giving me the best rest I'd had since......

Chapter 22

Sidney

It had been awhile since I took some personal time from work. In fact besides the Monday after my birthday, the last time I had any time off was back in March when the girls and I took a trip to the Bahamas for some much needed girl time.

The weather was not as tropical as I would have liked around that time but it sure beat the chill of DC with temps in the mid 70's the duration of our trip.

I remember stepping into our luxury three bedroom suite on Paradise Island which was so grand we hardly wanted to leave the premises. From the lavish pools that overlooked the perfectly clear turquoise blue ocean to the gorgeous Bahamian cabana boys that were there to cater to our every wish, we felt like queens upon a throne.

After spending the first day on the hotel grounds we decided to venture off and explore the island of Nassau. We spent the early part of the day at the local zoo which was one of my favorite places to visit no matter where I went. However, I could not get used to how freely the animals roamed the grounds there. You could be sitting on a park bench and look over your shoulder to a peacock standing behind you. We spent many moments calming Nina, who was startled more than once, giving us a great laugh and a good picture for the vacation album. We ended that memorable zoo trip by taking pictures with colorful parrots that were strategically placed on our arms and upon a hat atop our head by their handlers. This presented the perfect photo opportunity. This was one opportunity though in which Nina was eager to pass, but Jade and I managed to pull her in without the bird attached to her.

Later that night we decided to tour the aquarium grounds. The funny thing is we are still unclear to this day whether it was truly open or if we were trespassing during that time. There we met a few couples who roamed the tunnels which were completely made of glass tanks which surrounded us on both sides as well as the ceiling. They contained every fish imaginable as well as octopus, starfish, and sharks to name a few. We practically had to drag Nina along as she protested going through the dark tunnels stating we were setting ourselves up to be a case on the evening news by either being snatched by the boogie man himself or drowned by an underwater grave. Having the greatest imagination of us three, Jade was as eager as I to explore what the grounds had to offer and entered with no hesitation as she helped me pull Nina along.

I remember the three of us locking arms and suddenly running for what we thought was our lives when we saw the ceiling was dripping in the long dark tunnel made up of aquarium tanks with little light to guide the way. Because of the dripping, we feared it would burst at any moment taking us to certain under water death.

Returning to our hotel suite late that night, we were exhausted and decided to call it a night after showering and engaging in a little girl talk about the island boys.

The highlight of our trip however, came the following night when we were having drinks in the hotel's lounge and discovered, unplanned by us, that a swingers convention had come in from the west coast back home in the states and they were staying in our luxurious hotel of all places. We were pleasantly surprised at the turn our trip took from some much needed vacation time to some equally needed action.

As I lay in my bed now after taking a quick shower and changing into a silk ivory chemise with no panties, I touched myself as I daydreamed about that night when I met one of the participants who called himself Chase at the bar.

He was approximately 6'0" with dark curly hair, blue eyes, a fit physique, and milky even toned skin. Yes he was of the other persuasion. Although, I prefer a beautiful black man, I discovered my non-discriminatory nature back in college when I had my first experience with a white male by the name of Sean who looked like he stepped off of an Abercrombie and Fitch or American Eagle model ad and ate pussy like no other. In fact, if I didn't know better I would have sworn I needed an exorcism a few times because I just knew he made my head spin 360 degrees.

But anyways, looking at Chase now I could see he was in his early 30's or late 20's but confirmed he was actually 36, defying the black myth that whites do not age well. I learned he was an architect from Los Angeles and was in a relationship with a woman who was in the lifestyle but had to miss the trip. Lucky me, I thought as he smiled down at me showing a brilliant set of pearly white teeth.

After a few drinks I threw caution to the wind and gave my girls, who were bunned up on a couch in the corner of the lounge, the 4 1-1 before following him to the private beach that ran along the back of the hotel grounds. It was lit primarily by the lavish hotel lights but in the distance it grew darker as it was illuminated by the stars only.

I remember thinking this guy just might throw me in the ocean but upon gazing into his sexy crystal blue eyes which had me hypnotized at hello, I decided to take a chance and follow my vagina's carnal desire. Besides it had been awhile since I got some much needed gratification being as though I didn't have a man.

Walking along the white sandy beach drinks in hand, I remember how good the breeze felt as it kissed my neck blowing my hair in the night's slightly cool air. We chatted about our lives at home and I found myself intrigued by the fact that he had a small child with his girlfriend and that he planned to pop the question to her.

Despite engaging in the lifestyle as a single person, I always found it interesting that couples could share a deep love for each other yet actively participate in this lifestyle as well. I was especially intrigued by those who had no limits to the "bedroom play" with other couples and singles, especially those males who did not mind another man penetrating their wife or girlfriend. Yes there are rules to this thing and they vary from couple to couple.

If I ever became serious with anyone I doubt if I could continue to participate because I know myself and I have never been good at sharing much. Opening up my inner feelings to others more was another issue I was gaining progress with my therapist on.

As a matter of fact, I put my therapist's ideas into play just today when I decided to have a heart to heart with my best friend Nina as we walked the residential streets adjacent to her business. I did not shut down as I thought about the real danger that was brewing with a sexual predator loose in our city and wanted my girls to understand the seriousness of it all.

As Chase and I walked, I stopped for a moment when we reached a distance that was far enough to be private but still close enough for me to feel comfortable. He glanced up at the moon which was full tonight before staring into my eyes again with his baby blues. He stared at me intensely for a second, which felt like an eternity before palming my face in his hands and passionately filling my mouth with his warm tongue leaving me breathless when he finally released me from his grip.

I nearly gasped when he kissed my neck as he ran his finger tips up my summer dress before resting them just beneath my full bottom and lifting me into a position that straddled his perfect frame.

Palming my kitty in my bed now I thought about how good he smelled as the tropical breeze gave me shimmers of his intoxicating scent which was shower fresh mixed with a light scent that I could not put my finger on but salivated over none the less.

I felt safe in his arms as he slowly lowered me beneath the dark sky onto a bed of white sparkling sand. I felt a tingling sensation all over my body as he ran his hands up and down my thighs while continuing to passionately kiss my lips. His hands felt strong but soft as he explored my body running trails to my neck and back.

I did not protest when he pulled my panties down around my ankles and lifted my dress high above my head tossing it in a heap north of my head which was surrounded by a blanket of sand.

Feeling guilty for allowing him to do all of the work up until now, I broke our embrace to return the favor lifting his shirt above his head to reveal a perfect set of pecks and an amazingly ripped set of abs tossing it into the same heap.

I thought I heard the laughter of a couple who couldn't be too far in the distance perhaps engaging in their own private session as my tongue ran circles around his nipples.

Even the sound of the sea gulls could not break his concentration as he grabbed a hold of my waist with one hand and began unzipping his cargo shorts with the other revealing a perfectly shaven mid section and a rock hard member which he promptly covered with a condom he pulled from his pocket. This turned me on further as I loved a man who did not have to be reminded of safe sex. That goes without saying these days.

I tilted my head to the stars and closed my eyes, bracing myself for him to enter my pleasure pot only to feel a moist tongue press against my clit causing my hips to jerk forward and a loud moan to escape my now parted lips. It was no mystery to me that white boys gave good head so I was not surprised when he ate me like it was his last supper making sexy slurping sounds as he sampled my goodies in that wide open space. I was free of all inhibitions as I rotated my hips to match his rhythm and grabbed a hold of his soft curly tresses. He fondled my nipples as he feasted on my pussy juices sending electricity throughout my body.

Our chemistry was unmatched as the erotically exotic nature of what we were doing on that beach far away from reality hit home for me as I basked in the moment.

After multiple orgasms he finally freed me from the punishment his tongue was doing to my clit only to unleash a new sensation as he pushed my legs back behind my head and slowly entered me, my walls conforming to his every inch. He moaned and pumped slowly to a lover's rhythm as a bead of sweat formed on his brow before dripping onto my erect nipple.

I watched his image illuminated only by the moonlight as he made the most handsome fuck faces as he enjoyed my tight pussy which was dripping wet with desire.

I listened to the sound of the waves crash along the shore in the background as he rocked my boat. I did not flinch when his body stiffened as we came together in one long exaggerated fit of pure pleasure before he collapsed on the sand beside me.

We started giggling uncontrollably as we watched the sea gulls, competing for our attention, soar high above our heads. He pulled me on top of him and we playfully rolled around in the sand for a bit before returning to our luxury resort without a care in the world about our disheveled appearance.

This afternoon as I lay in my bed, I drifted off to sleep after masturbating to those fond memories of Chase that day on the Bahamian beach, happy to finally have a day of rest. With all that had been happening and the added stress of a serial killer on the loose in the nation's capital, I sure did need it.

I was happy I had the discussion earlier this afternoon with Nina about chilling from the lifestyle until this crazy person was captured. After that conversation and the reality of the situation which was buzzing at work, I needed the rest of the day off to relax. Now that things were picking up at work, who knew when that time would roll around again.

Chapter 23

Jade

Typical artist, I thought as I looked at my watch and waited for Jamal Wright to arrive at my gallery for the Friday night reveal party that I scheduled in his honor. I watched as participants of the events mingled, sipped champagne, and munched on hors d'oeuvres, appearing to not be the least phased by his now past fashionably late appearance.

Occasionally I would be interrupted by the buzz of my cell phone, which I had on vibrate so I could feel it when it went off, but the caller would hang up each time I answered, cancelling my hope that Jamal at least had the decency to call.

The calls were strange though because they started today from a private number and had been happening all day. I have to make a note to contact my provider and figure out how to block private callers on my personal line, I thought. Today was stressful enough without the calls.

My only satisfaction was that Devine was right here by my side helping me pass the time and keep the guests entertained with his charm and wit. The ladies appeared to be extra happy with him in attendance, making no secret about their more than obvious lustful thoughts.

I smiled when Nina and Sid snuck up behind me and tapped me on the shoulder before we exchanged warm embraces. I introduced them to Devine who gave them both a hug letting them know he had heard allot about them. They both grinned and gave me looks of approval and winks as he pardoned himself a few minutes later to greet a couple who he recognized from his gym.

"This guy is going to be the death of me" I murmured to them in regards to Jamal as soon as Devine was out of ear shot. I then shifted my weight on my heels and scanned the room.

"Oh don't worry," Sid said giving me a playful tap on the arm. "I'm sure he has a valid excuse," she continued smiling and scanning the room herself.

"Damn artists think they run the show," Nina whispered in classic Nina with attitude style. "He better get his ass here before the party rolls out on his cocky ass," she continued.

"I agree," I sighed nervously.

At that moment, I watched as a limo pulled up and Mr. Cocky made his way to the entrance. I grabbed the microphone and announced his presence as he smiled and took a bow. I glanced over and caught a glimpse of Nina roll her eyes at his gesture as Sid clapped with the crowd who acted as if he was right on time and not nearly two hours late as they cleared a path for him to further enter the gallery.

I managed a fake smile as he walked up to me and hugged me while whispering apologies into my ear. I slightly jumped as he brushed his lips across my ear lingering a little longer than I would have liked. I instantly hoped Devine was not in eyesight.

We had hit it off beautifully and after the gala last weekend I was feeling even better about his presence in my life. I had a few reservations about meeting his parents so early in our courtship, but that was quickly eased by the warmth and genuine kindness I felt in their presence. As a politician, his father had a commanding presence but I could tell he could be rather nurturing as I watched him cater to his wife who at first glance appeared shy but was especially friendly despite her shy nature.

We danced until our feet hurt that night and his father even stole a dance from me as Devine danced with his mother. It was a memorable night filled with fun and a rather productive networking experience as well as I gained contacts for my gallery among the crowd of participants who had gathered for the worthy cause.

Standing here now, I relaxed a bit as the man of the hour worked the crowd in a way that was magical, as solid inquiries were made about purchasing his work for both individual pleasure and large projects.

Devine winked at me from across the room as he now engaged in a conversation with Sid, Nina, and the couple from the gym. The rest of the night was uneventful and I was happy when it ended so I could spend a little alone time with Devine in the gallery.

We had not made love yet and that was the beauty of our newfound friendship. I felt no pressure and was quite happy with the pureness of what we had. He treated me like a lady and was slow with me. This was something I did not know I craved until this moment, yet here I was enjoying just the presence of him as we giggled and toasted to a successful night while sitting on the steps leading to my office in the back of the gallery.

"What are your dreams?" he asked turning our conversation serious for the moment.

"Hmmm," I said as I grabbed my chin and gave the question some thought before proceeding. "My dream is to live a peaceful life, productive in my ways, yet free and uninhibited in my spirit," I answered smiling while gazing into his beautiful eyes.

"I like the sound of that," he said as I rested my head on his shoulder and closed my eyes to reflect on the long day I had that was ending comfortably despite the trouble Mr. Wright could have caused by not showing up to his own event that I worked so hard to organize and promote.

Somehow none of that mattered though now as I enjoyed the presence of this man, something I had not truly enjoyed in years as my last relationship ended on bad terms. He was my high school sweetheart and the only man I really knew in the true meaning of the word before meeting Nina and Sid and trying out the lifestyle, which I had been curious about for some time.

Yes I had sexual encounters, including a few women, during our on again off again romance that lasted through college and up until I moved here about three years ago when we finally split for good, but I had never fully opened my heart up to anyone like I had Christian. He knew me when I was a tom boy long before my figure filled out. He was what I thought of as the love of my life and he was destined to be my husband but he decided I was not enough and thus broke my heart in the form of a threesome that did not include me. I often wonder if he purposely left clues so that I would find out despite the fact that our relationship appeared to be heading north at the time. It hurt that he could be so childish and outlandish after all that we had been through but such is life.

I had been taught by my mom at an early age to never chase a man and so I dust myself off and let it go despite the feeling of wasting so much of my life with him. In the end, I chalked it up as another one of life's lessons that I could grow from.

I was happy life brought me to DC where I met the closest girlfriends I had ever had, Nina and Sid, who treat me as if I have been a part of their sister circle from the beginning.

Sitting here with Devine now golden silence between us as we just sat and enjoyed being in each other's presence, I could not help but smile and be happy in the moment. I had my peace. I was finding productivity in my successful entrepreneurial endeavors. Freedom from all inhibitions within my spirit was surely on the horizon.

Chapter 24

Devine

The past few weeks had moved pretty fast yet I was not the least bit nervous about how our friendship had blossomed. Jade was a lovely woman with a good head on her shoulders and superb business sense that I found sexy to say the least.

I admired how she held her composure despite adversity when Mr. Wright decided to show up hours late for his own event. She was also highly professional when dismissing his obvious advances never once making me feel out of place among her friends, customers, or colleagues.

As I sat here looking at her face now, the moonlight illuminating the room, my heart was heavy with the disturbing news I had just received the day before. I wanted to tell her but could not form the words that would kill the mood of the moment we were sharing here on the steps of her gallery. Considering how fast things were moving, and despite her attempts at being open, I knew she still had a block up. I did not want her to feel this was a lie so fear moved through me as I knew the inevitable would have to be faced.

I knew I had to tell her but could not bring myself to spoil the moment as I sat here facing her and contemplating smothering her with kisses and my true feelings for her. I believed from the moment I saw her she was made for me. I never knew that could possibly happen to me but when it did I knew it was real. With the secret I now had hanging over us, I felt panic thinking about how abruptly this could all end once I uttered the words.

At that very moment my phone rang causing me to jump nervously. I smiled to play it off when I realized it was only my boy Keith probably checking to see what time I would be headed to our Friday night hangout spot to shoot pool. I forgot to tell him I had a change of plans this week after receiving an invite by Jade to the Jamal Wright art reveal party. I hoped she had not noticed the nervous gesture, I thought as I lifted my pointer finger indicating I needed to take this call but not before leaning over and kissing her cheek.

"What's up man?" I said as I answered the line.

"I can't call it my man, what's up with you? You headed down to the spot?" Keith asked.

He and I had been cousins and best friends practically since we came out of the wound. Our mother's were best friends having met in college and marrying brothers before moving to the same neighborhood in SE Washington, DC long before my dad became councilman Childs. Keith was a shorter light skinned version of me. We favored in many ways.

Besides the physical resemblance, we were both Scorpios with birthdays two weeks apart. Keith also played football in college separating from me briefly to attend school in Tennessee. His father was also overbearing trying his best to assert his beliefs and desires on his only son.

However, Keith was very strong minded and wasn't having it and made that fact known. He was his own man and pointed that out to his father whenever he could. He dropped out of college to play minor football briefly before also sustaining an injury that took him out of the league and drove him back to school knowing it would take a good salary to return to the DC area and live comfortably.

He continued his degree in Biology and went on to work for the coroner's office, an unlikely profession in my opinion knowing Keith. I couldn't understand his fascination with death given his love for life. I know that fascination had to increase with the serial murders taking place in the city.

He had one younger sister, Lynn who seemed to be content being a career student who never planned to leave home.

"I'm sorry man I forgot to tell you I had plans tonight. I'll have to catch up with you tomorrow," I said to Keith.

"She better be a bad one bro for you to be cancelling on me," he replied with a chuckle.

"She is," I simply stated looking up to smile at Jade who was pretending to busy herself with sipping on her wine.

"Alright man, I'll holla at you later bro," he said before hanging up.

"I'm sorry baby that was my cuz," I explained putting my phone back in my pocket, fear sweeping over me again about the information I was contemplating sharing with her.

A few nights ago I had received a surprise phone call from Mya who said we needed to meet and talk. At first I was skeptical because I had told her that I could not sleep with her any longer and our existence had to be strictly professional from here on out. We had this conversation in the past and she pulled the same stunt in an effort to seduce me back into the sac with her. I tried my hardest to explain the seriousness of this decision this time, blaming allot of it on the fact that she had a husband although I knew that wasn't really it. I was not into her nor could I go on this way knowing she wanted more and so did I, just not from her.

"You have someone huh?" she kept insisting at the time.

To that I let her know that was none of her business as she had a husband to answer to. When she called the other day I agreed to meet her in a public place, a local well lit park to be exact. When she arrived she looked exhausted and wrestled with the subject before coming out and telling me she was pregnant and was not sure if the baby belonged to me or her husband.

Stunned and in total shock I remember standing there blinking hard for a few trying to remember when this could have possibly happened as I stayed strapped up. However, my mind almost instantly went to a time almost two months ago when the rubber broke. She ensured me that there was no way she was ovulating at the time and not to worry. She wasn't on birth control because they gave her adverse side effects so I made sure I was very careful when I was with her with the exception of this one time. I was highly intoxicated and couldn't remember the details but that condom breaking wasn't something that slipped my mind and had stayed in the back of my mind in fact until this day. She continued the conversation stating that she planned to keep the child as she was getting up in age and had no children. In addition, she did not see how she could have an abortion and keep it from her husband.

I slightly chuckled at that remark being as though she had been keeping her affairs from him well enough over the years. She said I was the only one she was seeing besides her husband but I'd leave that up to the jury given her record.

I could kick myself at that very moment for being so stupid but being the man I am if the child is mines I will be there completely whether she liked it or not. We agreed that a DNA would be done once the child arrived.

Sitting here now looking at what had to be the love of my life and given the complicated circumstances, I could not help but hope that the child was not mine.

Chapter 25

Nina

Saturday mornings normally sucked as I would be coming down from an incredible hangover while rolling out of someone's bed or kicking someone out of mines, but today was different. Jay was flying into Reagan this morning so I left Brandon in charge as I took the day to spend with my baby.

As I stood here anxiously waiting for his flight to touch down and for him to walk through the terminal gate, I played with my smart phone searching for the record function. Damn technology can never be simple when you need it. It was no surprise that I did not notice when he walked right up on me planting a solid kiss on my lips that sent butterflies free throughout my body and caused me to nearly jump out of my skin.

"You scared me!" I said playfully punching him in the side with wide eyes as he laughed at my inattentiveness.

"Baby I just knew you were in for a shocker when I noticed you were all into that phone there," he said with that New Orleans accent as he continued laughing.

Instantly my emotions turned to a slight sadness as I realized I missed the opportunity I was waiting for.

"I missed you walking through the gate babe, I was trying to record the moment" I said with a sad face.

"Awww baby, I am sorry there will be other moments. If it makes you feel better you can still take pictures," he smiled kissing my forehead.

After a few shots, we strolled hand in hand through the airport and back to my Range Rover. Traffic was always heavy around the city and the weekend was no different as we inched along the parkway on our way back to my house so he could unpack and we could get our fun filled day started. Although I basically grew up in the city, site seeing was something I still did not mind as the city always had some new adventure around the corner.

Unfortunately, despite my protests we had a trip to the zoo lined up tomorrow. This was one adventure I'd gladly pass on but since my baby loved it compromise was in order this time around as long as he kept his promise to go roller skating with me later that night, which was reserved for the 30 and up crowd.

As we neared my townhome community, we were stopped by an officer who was directing traffic around an ambulance and a number of police cars that were blocking the one way street which led to my community.

An eerie feeling swept over me as we slowly followed the small path the cop had created as a detour in my Range Rover that ran perpendicular to a white van with the word "coroner" labeling its panel. We narrowly missed its doors being closed and secured by two men one large and the other smaller yet solid in stature. I recognized the smaller muscular built one from the high profile publicity that was being given to my friend Marcel Bennett's case. His name was Keith Childs and his picture flooded the local media recently. I believe he was related to Devine and the councilman from what I had heard but had not confirmed with Jade.

"I wonder what happened," Jay said eyes raised as we parked at the corner about a block away.

"I have no clue but it doesn't look good," I said glumly.

Walking to my block now we were stopped at the corner by the officer who was directing traffic. He apologized letting us know that no one could enter or leave the block until they finished gathering their evidence.

"What happened officer?" I asked trying to get a glimpse over his shoulder at the home they were leaving.

I recognized it as my neighbors, Gene, who was an openly bisexual and popular stylist to the semi rich and famous in the area.

"I'm sorry ma'am I cannot disclose any information at this time," the officer replied leading us away from the block as Jay wrapped his arms around my waste and helped me back to the car.

My heart sank as I glanced at the coroner's van as it made its exit from my block using the path the officers cleared. I did not want to think my neighbor Gene inhabited its space. I shook my head as I thought of him. We were not close but he was a good guy and great neighbor. He was in his mid thirty's and sported the most beautiful and well kept long dreads I had ever seen that he wore pulled back in various styles. He was average height and build with big Bambi eyes and small lips that always looked slightly pursed. Gene's personality was bold and fun yet lacked being overly flamboyant.

In addition, unlike many of my gay friends he was very personal about his private life and did not have allot of traffic in or out of his home which I had been in and it was in phenomenal condition to say the least.

He was open and energetic when out soliciting clients and attending local events when I ran into him from time to time, but when he was home he was quite the opposite.

I found him to be rather quiet in his home life yet still friendly as he would often wave to me and engage in small talk as we passed. My little "sister" Brandon would often flirt with him, later telling me that he hoped to get him a sugar daddy. It was no secret that Gene was living quite comfortably based on his clientele and the fact that most people in my trendy upscale neighborhood were.

As Jay and I walked back to the car, he offered to drive us to our next destination which at this point of confusion was unknown.

Chapter 26

Sidney

Kenny and I had just finished eating breakfast which consisted of my famous blueberry waffles, turkey bacon, eggs, and fresh brewed coffee when my door bell rang. I'd have to hit the gym double time to make up for the waffles I thought as I finished clearing the table and watched my brother hop into the living room to sit in front of the TV as I descended the stairs that led to my foyer.

I had reluctantly given him the information about his father the day before. I was reluctant because he was still going through so much physically, that I was unsure if this information would impact his mental state. He seemed to take it well ensuring me that he was happy to know our mom was happy at least once in her life.

Concentrating on answering the door now, I was curious to see who was on the other side as I wasn't expecting any packages. Furthermore, no one ever came by unannounced so I was especially shocked when I opened the door to see Nina and Jay standing there looking stunned.

"Hi guys," I said leaning in to kiss Nina on both cheeks and hug Jay as they entered the foyer, an obvious look of confusion on my face.

"I'm sorry girl to drop by unannounced but you won't believe the crazy shit, I mean stuff, going on in my neighborhood," Nina said as we made our way back up the small flight of stairs and into the living room where Kenny was trying his hardest to look over his shoulder from the couch as we entered.

"Heyyyyy lil brother" Nina sang as she scurried over to kiss his cheeks.

She adored Kenny and he could do no wrong in her eyes. She admitted that I spoiled him with him being a grown man and all but would stop short of telling me to quit especially when he was in her presence.

"Hey sis" he croaked clearing his throat in the process.

"Oh hell no, we need to call that doctor and find out why you still sound like that" she said with a look of concern on her face as Jay and Kenny gave each other some dap. He was the one man in Nina's life that Kenny always respected and never had one bad thing to say about.

"He was the one my crazy sis let get a way," was his response whenever Jay's name came up in the past.

To that Nina would roll her eyes and say "No honey he let all this get away humf!"

I took a seat on the couch beside Kenny as Nina and Jay took a seat on the opposite loveseat in the huge open space I simply called a living room because of my country roots. People here referred to it as a great room because of its massive size.

"So what's up?" I asked worry spreading in my mind as Nina never came by unannounced unless she had something seriously heavy on her mind and could not muster the strength to call first.

"We need to call mamacita over here for a family meeting," Nina replied glancing at Jay and shaking her head.

I reached over Kenny who now looked equally nervous and picked up the house phone to call Jade. She sounded as if she were still asleep but perked right up when I told her Nina and Jay were here and we needed her to come over as soon as she could for a family meeting. She said she would have to take a shower but would be right over as she did not open the gallery until early afternoon on Saturdays and had a little time to work with.

Nina helped me clean up the kitchen and the guys watched T.V. and had guy talk as we waited for Jade to arrive. Nina tried her best to make small talk as she rinsed and dried the dishes that I washed. I could tell she had something major on her mind but was trying to ease the anticipation by keeping the conversation up beat.

She told me about a few new toys that were on the market as well as the plans to attend the adult expo early next year in Vegas. I always attended the event with her as it gave us a chance to spend quality time together while supporting our friend in her business endeavors. Jade went with us the past two years and used the opportunity to score some new tastefully erotic paintings for her gallery as well as satisfying a few of her clients request for them as well. Nina always got really excited about the event toward the end of summer as we prepared to book our trip in early fall. Therefore, I was a little surprised that she was bringing it up this early in the game. However, I knew it had to be nerves about the conversation she wanted to have with Jade and I.

About an hour after we called her, Jade arrived with an expected look of worry written all over her face and settled in her body language.

"What's going on?" She asked as soon as we were all seated again.

We all turned to look at Nina who was doing that nervous habit she had of looking down and wringing her fingers as Jay rubbed her back.

"I called you all together to discuss the murders that have been going on in our backyard" she replied looking up and glancing around the room.

"Well those murders just got closer to my backyard. Jay and I watched the police and the coroner's office block off my neighborhood today. In fact they were at my neighbor Gene's house when we returned to the house from the airport. They wouldn't tell us anything or let me anywhere near my house" Nina exclaimed

127

tears now rolling down her face.

"What? How do you know it's related to what's been going in?" Kenny said his eyes now wide as he struggled to sit up straight.

"I don't but judging by the police presence and the fact that nothing of this magnitude ever happens in my neighborhood, I can't help but feel it's definitely related," Nina said a look of seriousness written on her face.

"Oh no Nina, this just got real," Jade said shaking her head, frown lines developing on her forehead.

"Let's not jump to conclusions, It could be completely unrelated," I interjected trying to be the voice of hope but I got an eerie feeling as well about this one. "Do you know if Gene was into the lifestyle?" I asked remembering the fact that the news reports over the past few weeks had stated the crimes were sexual in nature and that there was an undisclosed connection between the victims.

Because Marcel was known to be in the lifestyle, it would be probable that the connection may lie in the exclusive professional swingers' network. In addition, Nina had received the inside scoop from the investigation into Marcel's case that confirmed that it may well be tied to the underground lifestyle as well. The victim profiles illustrated this point.

Besides the fact that everyone knew that Marcel Bennett had been an active participant in the lifestyle, rumor had it that the couple that was found a few weeks before also had ties to the secret swinger's network. However, the news reports fell short of saying that the serial killer was targeting members of the secret society. We did not know much of anything about the other victims whose cases came earlier in the spring before it was known that a serial killer was on the loose. Furthermore, the FBI had been called in but they were not releasing the facts that led them to believe that this person was also a sexual predator.

All we knew was that the buzz was out, yet party hostesses like my girl Chantal were trying their best to convince their clientele that security was at an all time high and that safety was their main concern at these events. None of the known murders had carried over into nearby Northern Virginia or Maryland but everyone was on full alert nevertheless. We had not been to a single party since the big event at the Cartwright and planned to keep it that way until this maniac was caught.

"I don't think he was but you never can be too sure these days. We've gotten some surprises in the past," she said glancing at Jay.

"Huh? Don't look at me. That was my first and last experience, now you on the other hand Ms Lady..." he replied poking her in the side playfully.

"Mmmm hmm," she said giving him the side eye and giggling lightening up the mood some.

"Gene was bisexual though. However, besides Marcel he was the only victim that I know of who was so I guess that doesn't matter either," Nina continued.

"Well let's continue to play it safe and leave the parties alone for now and Nina please let us know what you hear as soon as you can get back to your place," Jade said standing. "Unfortunately I can't stay and talk because I have to make it to the gallery so here is my spare key in case you two need some alone time to unwind," she continued taking an extra key from her designer bag.

She then walked around to give us each a warm embrace, with the exception of Kenny who winced from the pain when she got too close, so she kissed him on the forehead instead. I thought I saw him blush. It was no secret he had a huge crush on Jade, calling her his cougar in secret. However, when he got around her he became nervous.

"Oh yes and I received your message the other day King and we definitely need to set up some time to talk business during this upcoming week," Jade said winking at him before preparing to make her exit.

I think his desire for her was further fueled by the fact that she was the only one in our circle that respected his wishes and called him King instead of his god given name Kenny. I think it made him feel like she was referring to him as her king. He cracked me up with that.

After Jade left we chatted for awhile about the announcement that Kenny made that he planned on taking our advice and working out a deal with Jade to sell his artwork. I was so proud of him for making that big step and contributed allot of that to the traumatizing event of him being shot and the newfound revelation that he inherited a god-given talent from a good man who loved our mother, his father. I hate it took that for him to realize he needed to get serious about his life and let his artwork be his ticket to success because my baby brother was definitely a skilled artist, but I was happy nevertheless that he was taking those positive steps forward.

Sitting here watching him bubble over with excitement about his latest project in honor of Pete, I wished he too had found his way out of the sometimes mean city streets of DC other than in a coffin six feet under but thanked him for leaving my brother with the blessing of a newfound respect for life and his gift of art.

Once he got better, we would have to go see Aunt Vivi. I hated seeing her in that nursing home looking the way she did because of my father and so did Kenny but she continued to have life flowing through her veins and that could have very much not been the case. She could have found her place with my mother six feet deep. I often wondered which would be worst but then when I had to watch my brother battle for his life, the selfish part of me was highly thankful and grateful for life in whatever form it was left.

After we discussed Kenny's future we talked a little bit more about the recent case with Gene speculating on what could have happened before we finally gave up and decided to wait to see what developments would come forward as a result of this new case.

We had no clue if that was in fact him being placed in the coroner's van. The details were beyond vague at this point. The whole incident was still new but eventually we knew the truth would have to reveal itself. Whether it was related or not we knew this person had to be caught in order for our city to be released from the fear we were all gripped with at this moment.

Exhausted from a truly eventful morning, Nina and Jay decided to take Jade up on that offer. They said their goodbyes before leaving Kenny and I to ponder over the unknown.

Becoming exhausted from the lack of information and our resulting speculation, we decided to make it a movie kind of Saturday filled with comedy and action packed blockbusters with predictable happy endings instead.

This was something we remained hopeful for despite our own saga which played like a horror film right here in our nation's capital.

Chapter 27

Devine

We continue to bring you the latest in breaking news! A well known local stylist Gene Harris is in critical condition today after he and a friend were found early Saturday morning in his home on Capitol Hill victims of a brutal attack. Kevin Little was pronounced dead upon arrival when the police found him and a then unconscious Harris early Saturday morning after he managed to make a distressed call to 9-1-1. Police are not saying if this incident is related to the ongoing serial homicide investigations that are taking place in the district. We will bring you the latest on this investigation as it becomes available.

Wow I thought as I watched the faces of the two victims flash across the news screen as I sat in my local coffee shop sipping a Latte and reading the morning paper which also had a headline on the front page about the very same story I was watching now. I did not know either gentleman but had seen Gene at a few events before as he was a native DC businessman and put together a few fits for my father, the councilman, in the past.

Buzz! Buzz! Buzz!

I felt my cell vibrating in my pocket and looked at the caller ID not at all surprised that it was in fact my father. He was probably calling to ask if I heard the news, I thought as I sent his call to voicemail deciding to call him back when I got in the office. I turned my ringer back on before slipping the phone back in my pocket while shaking my head at the city's latest homicide.

Although, I did not know them personally, I said a quick prayer for both men before I gathered my belongings and prepared to exit the coffee shop and walk the short distance to the gym. Life is short and taking the time out to appreciate it while also taking the time out to consider other people was something that I was determined to make a part of my daily living starting with this short prayer for Gene's recovery, the home going of the second victim, and peace for the rest of us in the city.

So far there was no motive and although they were not confirming, I could not help but get this sick feeling that the latest homicide and attempted homicide was related to the chaos we were experiencing at the hands of a serial killer.

Unfortunately Gene was in the hospital and in critical condition, but hopefully he would wake up and be the break this city needed.

I walked into the lobby greeting the front desk clerk as I passed. She too was engrossed in the morning news program on the flat screen mounted on the corner of the wall facing the reception desk. There happened to be another news flash across the screen about the latest event as I exited the lobby and entered the stairwell.

Climbing the three flights to my corner office at the gym, I paused briefly to answer my phone which was ringing again and wave to Mya through the glass wall that she was trying her hardest to get my attention through.

She had not been as regular at the gym during my hours but remained a permanent fixture nevertheless. I wonder how long that will last, I couldn't help but think. The thought of her being pregnant sent a fresh wave of nausea through my body.

Before answering, I briefly checked the caller ID and smiled when I saw the number.

"Hello beautiful," I answered trying hard not to sound slightly out of breath.

"Hello handsome," Jade replied sounding as se~ ~well. let~ it being this early in the morning.

I knew she made it a point to run each morning at~ she had been up for a few hours at least by now I thought ~ at the clock which read 8:00 a.m.

I sighed as I entered my office and took a seat at my desk which was stacked high with new membership information from the weekend. Business was booming and I loved it but could not understand why my staff could not file the paperwork where I asked.

"What's wrong?" she asked in a worried tone.

"Oh nothing babe, just work," I responded. "How was the rest of your weekend," I continued.

"It was good. I processed allot of orders from the Jamal Wright event and I have a potential new client, a local that I know will generate some much needed positive energy to this area," she replied sounding excited.

"That's great lady. Look at you doing your thing. You go girl" I said poking fun at her.

We laughed and continued chatting for a bit before I had to end the call to meet my client for a personal training session.

About an hour and numerous unanswered calls from my father later, I decided to head up to my office to call him back but was surprised when I got a ring from the front desk that he was in the lobby waiting to visit me. He rarely came to my gym but when he did make an appearance it generated a buzz from the clients who were no strangers to local celebrities but admired and respected the councilman for the big changes he made in the city over the years as well as his commanding presence. I knew I had to hurry down and escort him up before he was swarmed by supporters.

Entering the lobby, I noticed he wore a serious look on his face. This was not uncommon for the councilman who was accustomed to putting on his game face but the hard frown lines that became more evident the closer I got to him were.

"What's up pops?" I said a now puzzled look on my face as

135

Besides the look he wore on his face, his presence here alone .ne know something was not right.

"Hi son, can we talk in private?" He said shaking the hand of another member and forcing a smile as she congratulated him on the opening of the new center that would now become a reality due to the success of the gala.

I led the way back to my office and closed the door before pulling the blinds that gave me a bird's eye view of the club through the glass walls.

"What brings you here councilman?" I said sitting behind my desk as he smoothed his suit jacket and pants leg before taking a seat in one of the chairs in front of me.

"I have been calling you because there is something that is rather sensitive that I wanted to share with you. I did not want to do it here but time is of the essence so I have no choice." He said in his booming voice looking down at his hands for the first time that I could remember in forever.

He seemed nervous to be in my presence which I found odd because that was usually the reverse deal when it came to us two. Looking up briefly and seeing the frown lines now appearing on my forehead he adjusted himself in his seat before leaning slightly forward and continuing.

"There have been many unexplained murders in this city that appear to be the work of a serial killer. The latest tragedy involves a gentleman by the name of Gene Harris who is in a coma as we speak and another individual who is now deceased. You probably have seen it on the morning news by now?" he said questioningly and I could have sworn I saw beads of sweat beginning to collect around his brow as he adjusted his collar.

I nodded my head and sat silently waiting on him to get to the point because I had another client due any minute.

"Well I don't know how to tell you this son but Gene is your brother" he said putting his head down again and shaking it back and forth.

"What?" I exclaimed jumping out of my seat now.

"I'm sorry son but it was an affair I had about two years into

136

our marriage when your mother and I were having a rough patch" He replied his voice shaking as he stood up putting both hands in front of him gesturing me to sit.

I ignored the gesture but instead continued "what do you mean he is my brother pops? I'm 37 years old and you springing this shit on me?" I said.

All respect for him as my father went out of the window as I flailed my arms and walked to the corner of the room my back to him. I rubbed my temples doing the math as he tried explaining.

"Son your mother was aware and she forgave me. I paid child support for him and we gave his mother extra to keep it a secret as I fought to build my political career," he said walking over to me and placing his hand on my shoulder.

To this I removed myself from his grip and walked back to my desk turning only to ask one simple question.

"How old is he?"

My father sighed before stating "34 but..."

"He's the same fucking age as Tim?" I said my eyes getting wider at the utterance of my younger brother's name.

"Yes," he said putting his head down again.

"Does he know?" I continued referring to Gene.

He sighed before giving a single "No."

Shock and amazement couldn't do my feeling justice at this life changing moment.

"Pops I'm going to need a minute. I'll talk to you later," I said exhausted by the information that was given to me as I turned my back on him once more.

I had two brothers age 34. One from an affair my father had on my mother, who never did speak up for herself, with a woman who carried his child at the same time as she. One that I didn't even know existed but was clinging to life in a nearby hospital in my same city. One who grew up in my very own backyard that I knew only as a stranger who provided custom fits for my father, the councilman, from time to time. What a small and brutal world.

Chapter 28

Jade

Why does time seem to stand still when you have things to do and people to see? That was my thought as I counted down the minutes until I could finish up at the gallery and close my doors for the night.

It had been a long day filled with drama from Jamal Wright who was beyond being a pain in my side. His work was unique and he was highly sought after making him the deal of a lifetime but dealing with his personality was beginning to feel like babysitting a teenager in the early stages of smelling themselves. Him being located in Seattle and myself in DC made the matters worst as I found myself preparing for yet another trip out there to resolve logistical issues he kept creating.

Sometimes I feel as if he's not content unless he is making my life a living hell. I wondered if my soft spoken nature was also making me a victim of his charades. My day got even worst after speaking to Devine earlier. Our conversation was normal and ended upbeat. All was well, or so I thought, until I received an unexpected call back from him a few hours later. He seemed upset but when I asked what was wrong he said he could not go into it right then but wanted to meet with me later.

Although he insisted it had nothing to do with me, this made me nervous. As a woman I had heard that "we need to talk and it's not you but me" speech before. However, I agreed to do so only if we could meet on my turf in case I needed a drink afterward. He laughed easing the tension in the air and assured me that he just needed a listening ear for an issue he was presented with. I offered to cater a late dinner at my place and he agreed to meet me there at ten o'clock sharp.

Looking at the clock now, it was finally eight thirty so I decided to call my favorite little French spot La' Vie. By the time I closed up and rode the train there our entire meal was ready and packed to go. I winked at the girls who worked there and my favorite waiter Pierre before hurrying out the door to catch the next train to my stop which was close by.

When I entered my condo I quickly set the dining room table, pre-heat the oven to warm our dinner's contents, and set out a bottle of wine before rushing to the master suite to lay out something more comfortable to wear.

Not wanting to give the wrong impression as we had never been intimate, I decided on a simple silk kimono inspired wrap dress and black open toed flats. Doing another time check, I realized I only had about twenty minutes to freshen up and get dressed before Devine arrived.

I decided to take a quick shower since I had been running around all day. Once I got out of the steamy shower and oiled my body with my favorite scent, I realized I did not have time to pin up my long hair as I originally planned.

Therefore, I quickly brushed it and let its soft curls hang loose around my neck and shoulders. I then made my way to the kitchen to remove the contents of our dinner that needed warming from the oven and make our plates but not a minute too soon because suddenly the buzzer rang letting me know I had a visitor in the lobby.

After confirming Devine's arrival, I gave the signal to the front desk to allow him up and quickly rushed to the dining room to light the single candle that illuminated our French cuisine.

Hearing the doorbell now, I gave myself the once over and let out a deep breath before heading to the small foyer and opening the door. Standing before me was the tallest, darkest, and most handsome man of any woman's dreams. He looked even more gorgeous than the first time I laid eyes on him at the airport terminal.

"Hello baby, you look beautiful" he said hugging me as he entered with his free hand and pulling a bouquet of fresh red roses from behind his back with the other.

"Awww thank you," I said smiling and blushing as I took the flowers.

I inhaled their sweet essence as I led the way into the living room where I had him take a seat while I retrieved a vase to put the flowers in. After briefly arranging them in the crystal vase, I set them on the dining room table to compliment my table set up.

I watched with admiration as Devine stood when I entered the room, always the perfect gentleman, and pulled me close hugging me once more as I came near. This gesture along with the intoxicating scent of his cologne sent a wave of chills down my spine causing me to slightly shutter.

"Everything ok?" Devine asked a look of worry spreading across his face.

"Oh yes I'm fine," I said embarrassed at the repeat of that day in the coffee shop when I almost melted in his arms at the almost identical gesture.

"Are you up for a tour of my humble abode?" I continued smiling up at him for reassurance.

"Sure, that would be nice," he said taking me by the hand as I led the way.

I tried my best to give him a brief tour of my large 2000 sq ft luxury condo so that our food would not get too cold.

At the table now, we ate and made small talk. He complimented the chef causing an eruption of laughter as we both knew the food was catered.

I did not once mention the purpose of his visit tonight, giving him the time and space to start the conversation when he was ready. After eating a delicious meal, Devine helped me clear the table and wash the few dishes despite my protest.

Once we were done, we retired to the living room with a glass of wine. Sitting next to me on the couch, he gazed into my eyes as he stroked a loose curl that framed my face. I tried my best not to get hypnotized by the sight of his perfectly juicy lips as he began speaking.

"My father came by my office today and dropped a heavy load on me today," he began.

"I'm not sure if you heard but there was another homicide over the weekend that may be connected to the serial killings going on in the city," he continued.

"One man was murdered and the other is in critical condition in a local hospital," Devine then sighed, dropping his chin, and leaving a long pause unfilled afterward.

I used my index finger to raise his head and meet his gaze once more.

"Yes I heard about that in fact it happened right next door to my friend Nina's house," I said unsure of where he was going with this conversation and why he seemed so solemn and personally touched by the matter.

"Why? What is wrong?" I questioned my eyes raised.

I braced myself for bad news, judging by his body language and the call he made to me earlier, but I was unprepared for what he said next.

He went on to tell me how his father had an affair and the latest victim Gene was in fact his brother something he had no clue of until today. He then went on to give details about how his father hid Gene from him and his siblings and did little more for him other than paying child support.

I was surprised as his father was well respected in the community as a leader and family man. He did not strike me as the type that would hide a love child for so long only to bring the skeletons out of his closet when his son was hanging onto life at a nearby hospital.

I couldn't imagine the emotions that were going through Devine as I watched him nearly break down before me. He was unsure if he should reach out and go visit him or if she should lay low in the background to give his family space without the potential drama that the media could bring if they caught word of this.

According to Devine, his presence alone would spark controversy and peak the media's interest as the oldest child of the congressman who was rumored to have been with women in the past but all accusations were determined to be unfounded. This was a fact that especially bothered Devine because he felt his father not only lied to his supporters but he continued the lie to his own children throughout their lives making them feel they were one happy family that the media was just trying to slander because of his popularity with the citizens of the city.

I sat and listened as he poured his heart out not interrupting for a second as he vented.

It's funny how things can change and one's entire life can be altered over the course of such a small time frame, I thought hoping Devine would find peace with this newfound situation and the burden he was forced to bear as a result of his father's transgressions.

Chapter 29

Devine

This woman never ceases to amaze me I thought as Jade sat patiently listening to me vent about the recent turn of events. She did not once insult my father or make any hasty judgments for that matter. Instead, she listened and offered me the best advice one could ask for. That was to follow my heart and do what was best for me in my own time. Not my fathers' time and not even the potentially negative time that was stacked up against my brother Gene as he lay in a hospital bed clinging to life.

She told me guilt was not my burden to bear and I loved her even more for that because until I came over I felt nothing but guilt for not dropping everything and going to see him in the hospital given the new facts I was presented with.

This was no longer a stranger on the news but my brother. He had my blood flowing through his veins for thirty four years and I didn't even know he existed.

I continue playing in Jade's hair as I stroked her cheek and thanked her for the conversation. We had not been intimate but everything in me was yearning for her even more at this moment.

Lusting for the physical but fueled by the mental, I was beside myself in desire.

Not wanting to be too forward but unable to resist, I took both of her hands in mines and leaned in to kiss her soft lips sucking their sweetness individually. I kissed her for what felt like an eternity. My heart started beating fast as I palmed her face in both hands, kissing her deeply as our tongues explored one another.

I then kissed her neck passionately before breaking free and pulling her into my lap no longer able to fight my longing for her. Her body slightly tensed but relaxed into my frame as I held her close and engulfed her with another long passionate kiss.

I tilted her head back and inhaled her soft scent as I contemplated what her pussy would taste like. I felt my nature rise as I stroked her shoulder and pulled her closer into me unable to free myself from the mouth watering kiss as I filled her awaiting mouth with my tongue. I know she felt it too when she shifted in my lap, my manhood poking her in the bottom.

Unable to contain myself any longer I slid from under her perfect frame and laid her body down on the couch as I parted her slightly open legs and filled the space on top of her, continuing our passionate kiss. The temperature climbed as I rubbed her body down before breaking our kiss only to help her out of her dress and unbutton my own shirt which was clinging to me now, beads of sweat forming on my brow.

I took a moment to admire her perfectly erect breasts as she leaned forward running circles around my nipples as I rubbed the back of her neck then kissed her there taking in her soft scent. I then kissed her shoulders before laying her down once more and trailed soft kisses from her shoulders, around her neck, and down to her supple breasts taking them in my hot mouth one at a time.

"Mmmm, baby" she moaned letting me know I found her spot as I suckled on the areolas in a semi rough fashion, one that was not too soft but just hard enough to make them stand up in peak perfection.

My dick throbbed with swollen anticipation as I made my way down south following the trail of her flat stomach. Her back

146

arched with equal anticipation as I drew closer and closer to her hidden treasure. I came up only to look into her eyes as I circled her swollen clit through her silk panties which were getting wetter and wetter with each passing moment.

I watched her pretty face contort and listened to the sweetest moans before I decided she could not take any more and slipped her panties off in one motion replacing them with my wet mouth.

"Awwww" she gasped as I licked and sucked her swollen pink mound.

She then grabbed my bald head appearing to hold on for dear life. Next she began rubbing it as she made a series of beautiful moans and lifted her hips to meet my face time and time again. I grabbed her ass with both hands as I devoured her pussy which smelled intoxicating and tasted like the sweetest delicacy in any bakery. I could get addicted to this I thought as her juices wet my throat, the combination of that and my tongue making slurping sounds as I explored her treasure box.

Unable to fight the inevitable any longer, I scooped her up in my massive arms and carried her to her bedroom. She did not resist but instead gazed into my eyes with a look of pure submission as I placed her on top of her soft pink satin sheets.

My member was throbbing and standing at full attention, begging to be released as I unbuttoned my slacks and let them fall to the floor. Illuminated by only the moonlight I watched her perfect body laying there as I slipped out of my boxer briefs and moved closer to the side of her bed completely naked now.

I then climbed on top of her and from the time I first entered her, her pussy walls gripped me perfectly and I knew this was where I belonged. For the rest of the night we made passionate love and my problems were lifted if only for this night.

Chapter 30

King

Friday rolled around fast, I thought as I exited the building after my physical therapy appointment. It had been nearly a week since Nina dropped by with the news that the killings had moved into her backyard and what a difference a week could make.

Dude was still in a coma and from what the news was saying the other guy's funeral was set for tomorrow. It would be one week to the day after the incident.

Sidney was out front like clockwork waiting on me. I no longer relied on my crutches but used one to keep my balance as I slowly made my way to Sidney's beamer.

"How did it go?" She asked as I settled in the passenger seat.

"Good as it could, they work my ass in there and leave me feeling worst than when I came," I complained and then sighed.

"Aww it will be ok baby bro," she replied. "You are getting stronger and that's what matters the most," she continued.

"You're right about that sis, I told you I'm a warrior, a king in fact" I laughed looking at her.

She shook her head. "Well King, you have a big day today and

I want to let you know I'm proud of you" Sidney said surprising me by using my nickname.

She was referring to the fact that she was dropping me at my studio now so I could prepare for a meeting with Jade there later to discuss my art.

This was something I was still surprised I was down for. Even now it was still stressing me that boogie society may have a say so in what was good or not with my work. Each project was my baby and you know how a real man feels about his child. Shit there is nothing that can come between that bond and like a father and child relationship, there is no room for changes once it's done if you ask me. It is what it is. I paint it how I see it and that's the end of that.

Furthermore, I was still a little stressed about the fact that everything I once thought I knew about myself was no more as Aunt Jennifer laid down my real roots for Sid as I lay in that hospital bed.

It explained allot including why I never felt loved by Earl being his only son and all. Furthermore, I held onto a dark secret from my past and there was no way I was ready to let the cat out of the bag and shit especially knowing what I know now.

I loved my sister and she always had my back but the fact remained that she couldn't save me when he touched my penis through my superman drawers and made me do the same through his dingy smelly ass drawers. Sometimes he would pull it out and tell me "son this is what a real man looks like," before making me touch his nasty dick and smacking me hard for not doing it right. He would then stroke himself, drips of pre cum oozing from the tip as he made nasty noises.

At the time, I blamed it on the alcohol, the stench always oozing from his pores, but I've come to accept the fact that he was just a sick ass pervert. I wasn't his and he had no problem fucking with another man's child especially one that couldn't retaliate. There was definitely no way I could break that news to Sid. I'd take that shit to the grave with me first.

Besides being too embarrassed that I couldn't do anything to stop my manhood from being compromised even at such a young age, I knew she had already been through enough with that bastard and this would only further break her heart and put a dent in the progress she was making with her therapist.

Maybe one day I'll seek therapy like her but today I'm just taking it one step at a time.

As we neared my studio, Sid let me know that she had to return to work but if Jade could not drop me at home later that she would come back and pick me up. Riding the train was too much for me these days. I hated having to pull my big sister from her busy schedule at work to chauffeur me around but that was the hand I had been dealt courtesy of the single gunshot wound to my neck.

On a positive note, I was glad that Pete's cousin Mike had stopped talking about revenge and settled down. I was happy he was planning to return to school in the fall instead of potentially being confined to a jail cell for doing something stupid.

After some much needed self reflection, I realized it wouldn't change anything anyways even if we did have a lead on who this coward was. I'd still be required to do physical therapy three times per week, except from the confines of a maximum security prison, and he would still be six feet under.

As we pulled up to my studio, I kissed Sid on the cheek and thanked her for the ride. She insisted on helping me upstairs but I declined, letting her know that the elevator was cool. I had about an hour before Jade was due to arrive so I would spend it tidying up my studio the best I could and arranging my work. After Sid drove off I hobbled my way to the elevator and up to my studio to do just that.

Five minutes before the hour my cell rang. I checked the caller ID hoping it wasn't another call from Kim who had still insisted on calling me every day to check up on me. I had not been returning her calls so she left continuous long winded messages in my inbox. They were starting to get hostile so I knew I would have to face the music sooner or later. I was happy to see it was Jade right on schedule.

"Hey lady," I said smiling as I answered the phone.

"Hey King, I'm out front can you buzz me in?" she asked referring to the box out front.

The call feature never worked forcing visitors to use their cell phones to notify their people when they were out front and needed to be buzzed in. There was a security guard at the desk in the lobby but he wasn't in direct view of the front entrance so he never paid much attention to whether or not people were out front waiting to get in. Even if he was, his lazy ass was sure to ignore them anyways.

"Sure thing" I said pushing the button on the panel as I hung up the phone. A few minutes later she was at the door. When I opened it, she breezed in dropping her briefcase on the small table situated near the closet sized kitchen to the left as she entered the studio.

Besides the small dinette, the only other furniture I had in the studio was a desk that I used to sketch and hold supplies, a chair, futon, and a television mounted on the far corner of the wall. The room contained the bare necessities for times when I was confined to the studio for longer than expected as I worked on my craft.

"Whew sorry I'm late" she sighed as she came over and kissed me on both cheeks.

"Late?" I questioned. "You said noon so that makes you right on time" I said looking at the time on my cell for confirmation.

"Sweetie when you are on time you are late" she said a look of disbelief on her face. "Have I not taught you anything" she smiled taking note of my confused expression as she sat down on the futon. To that we both laughed.

For the next two hours we went over some of my pieces. She explained to me how the business worked and gave me her ideas for marketing my specific work and getting me exposure in the city and surrounding areas. This included some late night gigs that were right up my alley giving me exposure and access to fun at the same time. With her agreement, I would retain all rights to my pieces. I would create prints from some while selling others in their original state as one of a kind masterpieces. This excited me because I always dug originals and despised prints.

Besides, I was learning that these rich people actually respected the craft and paid big money for artwork from urban cats like myself. In some cases they would buy sight unseen as Jade illustrated to me through some examples of artists she had been involved with lately like that cat Jamal Wright from Seattle that everyone in the art world was buzzing about lately.

He had become a success almost overnight. In my opinion, he couldn't touch my skills and from I heard he was cocky as hell so I imagined if he made it what would become of me given this opportunity.

We finished our meeting on a high note with an impressive contract that Jade presented to me. I didn't bother getting a lawyer because she was like family and I knew she had my best interest at heart so I wasn't concerned in the least.

During our meeting I had to turn my phone off because Kim called me at least ten times and left eight messages. At one point I had to briefly put a halt to our meeting so I could let Jade know what was going on and apologize for the interruptions. This chick was beginning to be stalker material which was odd to me judging by her party girl attitude. I figured she knew what it was and was down to just have fun. Now that I was getting my life on track and with the deal of a lifetime in hand, there was no way I was going back to a shorty of her caliber. I had to get my priorities in order and women were not at the top of that list. However, when I do settle down she has to be right on all levels.

I was happy Jade didn't flinch with the constant interruptions. In fact her phone rang quite a few times too but she kept her focus on me and I was digging that. I found myself watching her closely as she spoke. She was sexy no doubt but her business persona was something I never experienced in a woman and I wondered if that was part of my attraction to her which was increasing which each passing moment that I spent alone with her.

I tried my hardest not to check out her tight waist and beautiful curves as she leaned forward on the table to point out important terms and clauses in the contract. I got a whiff of her light floral scent when she sat back, flipped her long hair, exposing her long neck, and smiled handing me the pen. Word from my big sis was that she got a new man but that dude didn't mean anything to me. In fact, he would have to step to the side real soon because when I make it where I want to be, she will be on my arm cheering me on. I was sure of that. Jade Davis, now that has a nice ring to it I thought as I took the pen and signed my name.

This was the first positive step toward a bright future. I could see it. I can only go up from here and as far as I could tell the sky has no limits. Word....

Chapter 31

Nina

Over three months had passed since the last connected murder had taken place in the city. According to the news reports, the last known body was that of a young girl in her early twenties found in a dumpster in a SE alley by an unsuspecting sanitation worker back in July. She was completely naked, bound, and gagged. This was a detail that most of the victims had in common, a detail that wasn't released until this incident. This case seemed to be the last straw for the local police and FBI who were feeling pressure by leaders and the community as a whole to release more details about the investigation including a possible profile of the suspect.

Until that point most information had been up for speculation. I did learn however, that most of the victims had been sodomized. The item of choice had been left inserted in their anus. This was more confirmation of the theory that the suspect was a sexual predator.

The sodomy detail had not been leaked to the public but given to me by a friend who was a detective and for as long as I could remember has wanted to get in my panties. He knew I was close to

Marcel Bennett and fed me the information, details that I had not told my girls or Jay for that matter.

All were fearful and I did not want to add anything else to that long list of worries. Jay was making it a point to come up here more often and sent for me every chance I could get away.

The best and brightest from around the country had been brought in which included the nation's best known criminal profiler. The result was a profile that stated the area should be on the lookout for a male in his mid to late twenties. He could very well be bisexual or gay. He would most likely be a native to the area but a loner who totally submerged himself in his career. Most likely he did not drive and had a passive aggressive personality. Growing up in DC from a young age, I knew that profile didn't do a whole lot to exclude a large portion of the population. Shoot I could name quite a few who fit that profile to the tee.

A majority of the city's hope lie in the hands of my neighbor Gene, the sole known survivor of the attacks whom we found out was actually the brother of Jade's new beau Devine. However, that hope all but vanished when he woke up from his coma three weeks after the incident without a trace of memory of the event or the time leading up to it. He had not been back to his home since but instead had been staying with Devine who ensured he got the best physical therapy possible from a private source.

Apparently the media still had not gotten word of the relationship between the two but instead had been posted up at his mother's house trying to get a glimpse of him since he left the hospital. They narrowly missed him dressed in disguise as he exited the rear of the hospital upon his release.

It was now October and since they had found the young lady in the dumpster, the murders that had gripped this city starting in late spring seemed to have ceased as fast as they had started. Despite that fact, the girls and I had not been to a party in months.

Honestly, I wasn't missing them much with Jay in my life in full force now. Despite the distance, we were getting serious and knew eventually something would have to give if we were going to move forward in our relationship. Someone would have to relocate.

I was hoping that someone would not have to be me.

Besides, given the nature of his career as an architect, he could manage his business from any major city in the U.S. Over the past few months, we had spent allot of time back and forth visiting one another which was hard with us both owning our own business and all.

Like now, I was in Houston visiting him. Fall had not set in here like it had at home so I instantly had to start stripping out of my layers of clothing as I stepped out of the airport early on a Friday morning to pick up my rental car in the parking garage. Even at this early time of day, the sun was beaming down hard and the air was warm with a very mild and comfortable breeze.

Jay had a business meeting that he could not get out of so I didn't get my usual greeting as I stepped out of the terminal. Instead I had to rent a vehicle and make my way to his home on my own. I had been here plenty of times so I had no problems finding my way.

The red BMW 328i I picked out at the rental car stand was little and cute. It wasn't what I was used to with the large comfort of the Range Rover but after driving it the short distance to Jay's home, I understood why Sidney loved her drop top beamer so much.

Pulling up in his circular driveway in the Westheimer neighborhood located in the Galleria portion of town, a prominent neighborhood in Houston, TX, I was impressed as usual at how well manicured his lawn was. Knowing Jay and how hands on he was, despite his busy schedule I knew he had taken direct responsibility for a portion if not all of the landscaping to his property.

He had a rather large brick home, huge for a single person in my opinion, which sat on at least an acre of land with a guest pool house in the rear that was almost identical to his home. Looking at the exterior, it was just a scaled down version of the main house. Back in DC you could never get a home sitting on this much land unless you planned to live far out in the suburbs of Northern VA or one of the suburban counties of Maryland.

I parked the beamer in the circular driveway and made my way to the huge door where I found the key under a porch ornament.

As instructed, I let myself in being careful when inputting the exact digits he gave me to disable the alarm system. When I heard the series of beeps giving me confirmation that it was disabled, I ran back outside and grabbed my bags from the trunk of the car and made my way back inside.

Once inside, I headed for the bedroom to shower and slip into the new red lace teddy I bought for my visit along with the matching red pumps. My boo let me know that he would be making his way home as soon as his meeting was over to spend the rest of the afternoon and all weekend with me.

These trips could not come quick enough as my body ached for some sexual healing in the worst way. Now that I was here, I was on the peak of eruption.

I knew this had to be true love because in the past I would not hesitate to satisfy my desires. He or she was just a phone call away in my handy little black book. Now I had to be happy with a dildo and some lube. If that didn't work my first love of self could be counted on to do the trick. Shit, I could masturbate myself to ecstasy or a state of frenzy if need be in record time at this stage of the game.

In the master bathroom now, I got undressed and stepped into Jay's huge Roman shower. I couldn't help but think of how its massive size could be of benefit. It could probably fit six people easily. I know he wasn't down for the lifestyle but if he ever wanted to give it a try this shower would be the perfect setting for a sexual oasis, I thought as I began touching myself as the stream of water flowed down my clit.

I imagined Jay's hands replacing mines as I lathered my cloth with soap and sponged my body down. I watched the soap run down my legs as it was washed away by the steady stream from the high pressured shower head. I leaned my head back and allowed the warm water to run down my neck. I closed my eyes and concentrated on the trail it made down my back and around the curves in my perfectly round bottom.

I thought my mind was playing tricks on me when I felt a pair of strong hands wrap around my waste and the softest set of lips on the nape of my neck.

"Hey beautiful," he whispered in my ear in a seductive tone as he pressed my body against the shower, his steel suggestively pressing against my ass.

Instantly, my juices flowed as he lifted my right leg entering me from behind slowly and without warning. In and out he slowly pumped filling my walls with deep penetration. My body shuttered as I listened to the sexy sound of his heavy breathing in my ear which increased with each stroke. I gasped as he pulled out and turned me around pressing my back against the shower as he kissed me long and hard stroking his glistening dick with his right hand before flipping the valve off with his left hand and scooping me up.

He continued kissing me as he walked me to his king sized bed and laid me down dripping wet and all. My pussy throbbed with anticipation as he took my foot in his mouth and began sucking. From the soles of my feet, to the top of my head, and everything in between he took the next few hours to explore every inch of my tall frame leaving no spot behind. My body trembled uncontrollably with orgasmic pleasure and by the time he entered me again I was overflowing and dripping wet. My pussy walls contracted as she beckoned him to make her cum.

The rest of the afternoon was a blur and before we knew it we had collapsed and fell into a deep sleep. Our bodies succumbed to the demand we had placed on it with the rest of the morning and afternoon being dedicated to both making love and fucking.

Sometime late in the evening I woke up to use the restroom and grab a light snack from the kitchen. When I returned, Jay was still fast asleep. He had not stirred hardly an inch when I untangled our bodies.

I decided to grab the remote from the nightstand for the flat screen television and see what was on. Flipping through the channels trying to find a police or criminal show, which happened to be mines and Sid's favorite when we had down time, my attention was caught by a photo that was being flashed on one of the specials. My jaw dropped and if I had not known better I would swear I stopped breathing momentarily. I had to blink hard twice to be sure I was awake and then I turned the volume up.

The sight before me and its content was something that would change my life forever. Instantly, I picked up the phone. There was only one number I could call without sounding crazy. I had been under a great deal of stress lately and I prayed this was just something in my mind, a figment of my imagination, hundreds of miles from home.

Chapter 32

Sidney

It had been raining all day. Thank god I had taken this Friday off. As I stared out the bay window of my bedroom, I watched the people scanter along. Many were running to catch their busses, cabs, or trains to get inside where it was warm and dry.

It had been an unpredictable fall thus far with temperatures dipping very low and then skyrocketing within 24 hours to record high temps. Today was one of those chilly days topped with rain that had not let up all day.

I had spent most of the day inside helping Kenny get ready for an event he was headlining tomorrow night at an artsy café downtown. Jade and I would be there to support and cheer him on as he painted a free style piece in front of the audience.

These past three months had been wonderful for him. He signed a contract with Jade for his artwork and had sold quite a few for a hefty price tag. He was now gearing up to take classes in the spring to fine tune as well as gain new art skills. This was something he would not have ever entertained just a few short months ago. He had also opened a business account and worked heavily with

Jade to brand an image for himself which was taking off. He had long been known in the city in the underground art scene but was blossoming into a well received mainstream artist as well with a bright future ahead.

I was not at all surprised at how quickly this was all happening for him. He was talented and smart. I had told him this time and time again. He just needed to focus and unfortunately it took the life altering shooting event to change him for the better.

He had even been talking about buying his own place sometime during the first part of next year. I was not too enthused about that idea because I wanted him to be careful about his decisions and save as much as possible but he was grown and like he said he was a man and had to make his own way so I was happy for him.

Furthermore, his physical therapy had moved along better than expected and with the exception of the physical scar he was almost back to complete normalcy. The way he moved I wasn't surprised at that fact either. My brother hated to be confined and he hated depending on people, myself included, just as much. However, he knew my fussing was out of love and he could never really be an inconvenience to me.

Sitting here staring out of the window now at the people moving about their business, I could not help but think about how busy this weekend was going to be and wondered if I had committed to do too much.

We had not been to a party in months with the serial killings happening in the city even though it had been over three months since any new killings had been linked to the incidents. Although Nina was out of town visiting her man, Jade and I had decided now would be the time that we come out of hiding and attend a Halloween masquerade party that was scheduled for tonight at Chantal's place in Maryland.

This event got bigger and bigger each year. However, with all that had happened in the District of Columbia over the summer and the grip that this monster had on the city, there had not been allot of buzz about the event until this past week.

Although the murders had been confined to the city, the

surrounding areas of Northern Virginia and Maryland had shared in our fear as the three connected their communities and shared ties in many ways. Jade and I had just decided to go last night as we discussed plans for Kenny's event.

With no real male prospects still the release was well past due for me. Countless hours in the gym with my trainer and masturbation was no longer cutting it. I needed the real thing.

Although she was hot and heavy with Devine lately, Jade still had an appetite for unconventional sex that she was not willing to share with him quite yet.

"Ladies he won't understand," she had said to Nina and I one day during our girl's night out at our favorite French restaurant and hangout spot La'Vie.

"You never know," I had responded and high fived Nina who turned her lips up and shook her head in agreement.

"Most men would love the opportunity to have a mamacita that was down for whenever, wherever, and whatever," Nina continued laughing as she sang the last three words of the famous lyrics.

We all joined in the laughter including Jade who was nervous about the subject because she had began developing deeper feelings for Devine.

She said he had shared allot of intimate things with her early on including the fact that Nina's neighbor who was the only known survivor of the city's attacks, was actually his half brother from an affair. This was something that could send the media in a frenzy and spell the demise of his father's political career yet he trusted her with the details. She didn't even want to tell us as her best girlfriends about the relationship but Nina, who could talk the panties off of a nun, was able to get it out of her after hearing the rumor from a trusted source inside of the investigation.

Ring! Ring!

My thoughts were interrupted by the sound of my cell which was followed up by the sound of thunder cracking, stirring both the earth and my insides causing me to jump.

"Ms. Davis speaking," I answered not bothering to look at the caller I.D.

"Hi sweetie, you ready for tonight?" Jade asked with the obvious hint of a smile in her voice.

"Not quite but I will be" I replied, that same smile in my voice too I was sure.

"Well I have my outfit together and it is perfect. I just came from Nina's boutique where she had the cutest mask and wig to complete my look," she said getting excited.

I was wondering how she planned to get all of that naturally long hair under a cap to put on a wig but I didn't ask. Instead, I made my way to my closet where I kept my various costumes locked away in a storage trunk in the corner. I had numerous masks from previous parties and events so it was just a matter of choosing one. I knew the same held true for Jade but she loved the thrill of shopping so it came as no surprise that she found something new to wear tonight on such short notice.

We made small talk as I searched through my treasure box for the perfect pieces to complete my look. While placing a small accessory box on the shelf of my closet our call was interrupted by a beep. My hands full, I was unable to check the caller I.D or click over so I decided that whoever it was would have to settle for a call back.

When I emerged from my closet Kenny came in to show me a couple of fits he had chosen for his event tomorrow to get my attention. Both had that half prep half urban chic look I enjoyed on the guys. I could not stand baggy pants, Nike boots, or Timberlands. These were all items of choice that Kenny inherited growing up in DC. However, his country roots showed sometimes when he was trying to impress and I loved that.

With his tall athletic frame and freshly designed long dreads, the canary button up, dark green vest, thick black rimmed non prescription designer eyeglasses, and fitted dark denim jeans were going to suit him well. That's the outfit that stood out to me as my choice and of course he obliged.

I then spent the next few minutes describing his choice for the event to Jade who seemed overwhelmed with Joy at the transformation that was taking place with Kenny. However, this was not before trying my best to lie to him about our plans for the evening, describing it as just a Halloween party to get him out of my room.

Jade chuckled.

I was grown and so was Kenny so she didn't understand why I didn't just tell him the truth about the sex parties.

"Ok sweetie don't be surprised if you run into him at an event one day especially now that he is moving up in the world and meeting all types of people," she said in a convincing tone but I wasn't ready for that.

After talking for a short time more and finalizing our plans for the evening, I decided to take a long hot bath and get ready. Tonight was sure to be full of excitement and I couldn't wait to see what treats were in store for me. It was a long time coming.

Chapter 33

Jade

Hopping in my Mini Cooper to go pick up Sidney, I realized I had two missed calls from Nina. I was a bad liar so I decided to call her back later to keep from telling her about the party. Sid and I had discussed this briefly and we did not want her worrying while she was away on her trip visiting Jay who deserved her undivided attention.

He was a great guy who catered to her every wish despite living in Houston. No matter how far away he was he loved my girl that's for sure. They had been seriously reconnecting. I could tell they were not just living the fantasy of a childhood romance and if you ask me despite Nina's protest, I see wedding bells in their future.

She was probably just calling now to let me know she had made it safely and that's all that mattered. I had taken her to the airport early this morning and had told her to call me when she touched down. Knowing Nina, she had gotten caught up in that good penis and was just getting a chance to call.

DC traffic was a nightmare as usual on a Friday night. It was bad on any day and that's why I caught the train as much as possible.

When I arrived at Sidney's she came out before I could call. She tossed her bag in the backseat and kissed both of my cheeks in our typical girlfriend fashion and we were off. Normally we would meet at the metro but since it was just the two of us and this party was on a Friday night making us pressed for time, I offered to pick her up. I was glad I did because we were running late.

When we got to Chantal's home in the suburbs of Maryland, she greeted us at the door hugging us closely. She had on a beautiful gold and black satin mask with a one piece matching cat suit. When we stepped in the foyer, I took in the awesome decorations that were completely befitting of both the Halloween and sexy theme for the evening.

The great room right outside of the foyer was illuminated by strategically placed jack-o-lanterns only. There were spider webs on the ceiling and scantily clad mannequins painted with frightening make-up in various corners of the room. The bottles at the bar that was set up in the middle of the room were set up to look like potion bottles with a large pot to simulate witches brew.

The DJ was a frequent guest and patron of Chantal's events coming from behind the booth from time to time to do more than spin records. Nina and I had been with him a few times in the past. I must say he definitely lived up to the hype the females who positioned themselves around his booth waiting for their opportunity to experience him gave him.

I glanced around the room and noticed it was more crowded than we expected.

"I have not seen you in forever" Chantal squealed coming from behind the table, where she was collecting donations, to give us hugs when she saw our driver's licenses.

At first she did not recognize us in our costumes. Checking identification was something new they started as a security precaution given the attacks that had taken place.

"I know," we both said at the same time looking at each other and giggling.

Mingling with the crowd now, I admired all of the beautiful masks that people wore. The requirement of the party was that

168

everyone wore their own unique mask to compliment their costume. There were masks in all shapes, sizes, and colors.

When we saw a lady sporting a red teddy, red and black mask, horns, and a red devil's tail on her rear, I instantly thought of Nina who would have looked perfect in the costume.

The DJ winked at me as we passed his booth on the way to the bar. It had been awhile since I had been in this setting and now that I was here I doubted very seriously that I was ready for him. In fact, Devine had invaded my thoughts yet again and I wondered if this would be considered cheating since we never discussed exclusivity.

A few songs later, Chantal took the microphone and announced the start of the costume contest.

As we gathered in a circle, my attention was caught by a tall man wearing all black wearing a white full faced mask. He was tall and had a solid physique. His well defined pecks showed through his nicely fitted v-neck cashmere sweater. Despite being more fully clothed than other males in the room, he stood out as noteworthy. We decided to not participate in the contest. Frankly, our confidence level went down with the absence of Nina who was definitely the party starter in our group.

We cheered along with the crowd as the women showed their stuff and bent over in their costumes followed by the male participants. Our applause determined the winner. The standout female was a lady dressed as a sexy version of Wonder Woman complete with blue thong and red cape. The guy was a Puerto Rican male dressed as Tarzan with oiled up six pack abs, brown suede thong, and a matching mask. He sported long dark curly hair and shells around his ankle and neck.

After the contest and the playground rules were read for this evening's festivities, Sidney and I began dancing as my song filled the air. Couples started slow grinding and removing all or part of their costumes in preparation to retire to the various parts of the house where sex was not prohibited yet strongly encouraged.

Sidney was approached by the Puerto Rican gentleman who had won the contest earlier. He whispered something in her ear that obviously sparked her attention because before I knew it she let me know she was heading to a different part of the house with the gentleman. However, she wanted me to make sure I stayed within a close enough range that we could meet back up easily throughout the night. I agreed telling her to have fun and not worry about me.

A few minutes after Sidney left I engaged in a conversation with two females dressed as sexy rag dolls. However, I was not interested in female company either tonight so I excused myself to wonder up stairs and see if anything interesting was occurring.

Standing in the doorway of one of the upstairs bedrooms I watched as three guys had their way with a sexy, tall, and slim woman who had ass for days. She was taking turns sucking a tall light skinned black male as well as a Caucasian male while the third, a dark skinned solid guy who looked like he played for the NFL, punished her pussy from the back. I started getting wet as I watched her wetness glisten all over what had to be a magnum sized rubber that was secured tightly on his huge dick. He pumped and sweated as I listened to her ass cheeks smack his thighs.

I continued watching as a white female approached and began tongue kissing the white male, most likely she was his partner, and then sat on the bed and started massaging the back of the female who was trying her best to continue sucking the two men while her head rocked back and forth frantically from the thrusts she was receiving from behind.

I closed my eyes briefly to imagine what it would feel like if she were I when I suddenly felt two pair of warm arms wrap around my waist and pull me tight. I jumped to see the gentleman from downstairs. Although he had on a mask, I could see by the lines on the sides of his face that he was smiling underneath that mask. I playfully pushed him away wondering if he guessed what I was daydreaming.

The sounds of pure bliss were escaping the five people who were all heavily involved in play now. It was written all over their faces that they were all on the verge of sexual eruption. As the sweet sounds of release escaped them one by one my heart began to beat fast, unable to hide my excitement due to the erotic scene before me.

The unknown gentleman took me by the hands and led me out of the room and down the stairs back to the great room where bodies were closely intertwined. They seemed to be enjoying the foreplay, compliments of slow grinding to the sensual tunes the DJ was playing to set the mood.

I sighed as the tall stranger took me by the waste and pulled me close as we began our own dance session. His smell was hypnotizing and almost familiar. I laid my head on his chest and began grinding with the beat as he rubbed the small of my back. No words were exchanged between us instead we lived in the moment, innocent as it was.

Chapter 34

Nina

I had been calling both Sidney and Jade to no avail. This caused worry and panic to build up in me.

I woke Jay and explained what I saw to his disbelief as well. He wondered if I was sure and if I may have been suffering from jet lag or perhaps sleep deprivation from the long hours I had been putting in at the boutique. I shook my head at this notion but after having a few hours to think about it I was beginning to doubt myself as well. However, after replaying the special over and over again in my head as well as the image that flashed across the screen crystal clear, I knew I could not doubt myself and had to make sure my friends were not in danger.

The fact that they had not been answering my calls increased my fears. This rang especially true with Sidney who would have normally called me back by now. She didn't have a date tonight that I knew of and Kenny was doing great from what I could see even with the newfound revelation about his father. He seemed to be taking the news well and moving forward with his plans to get serious about his gift. He had no further complications from the shooting that I was aware of and if I remembered correctly his event was not scheduled until tomorrow night so it was strange that Sidney was not answering.

For the next few hours I tried calling them both again. To my surprise both phones were now going straight to voicemail. I also called Kenny to no avail.

Pacing back and forth now, I wondered if I should call the authorities or if Jay was right and this was just one big misunderstanding. Until I heard from them, the worst continued to consume me.

Chapter 35

Jade

This guy was mind blowing. Not once during our dance did I think of Devine standing here with me which was a first since I had met him.

During the rest of the evening he did not once attempt to have sex with me which was strange given this atmosphere. Instead he kept the silence between us going until the end of the night when he invited me back to his hotel suite. I hesitated knowing the dangers of leaving with strangers but if he got into this event as a single male, I knew he had to be known by the hostess.

Having got his information I went to find Sidney and pass it to her along with the keys to my Mini so she could get home. After much protest from her, I assured her things would be fine and I would check in with her first thing in the a.m. before slipping out the front door.

At the Cartwright hotel now, the same luxury hotel that we went to the lavish event back in the early part of the summer, I was impressed by the lavish penthouse suite equipped with a huge closed in deck that had an awaiting hot tub. I didn't have a swimsuit so I agreed to strip down to my lace bra and thong set to join him in the hot tub where he was wearing nothing more than boxer briefs, his large print making my mouth water.

It did not take things long to get heated up in the hot tub which illustrated to me that he was a private person after all and most likely a newbie to the party scene. This fact briefly made me nervous but then I recalled that no one got an invite as a single male unless they personally knew Chantal and were thoroughly checked out and approved.

He rubbed my thighs and circled the areolas of my breasts through my bra as he kissed me deep the steam igniting our passion. Our hands explored one another for the next few minutes before we decided we could not take it any longer.

So we dried off and I followed him to the bedroom. Although it was dark I could make out his perfect silhouette as he stripped down to nothing. He grabbed a condom from the dresser and slid it on his rock hard member before approaching me.

I stood at the edge of the bed in nervous anticipation of what was next. He then walked up to me and firmly pressed his body against mines before lifting me effortlessly while wrapping my legs around his waist. He then turned and sat on the very same edge of the bed near where I was standing when he lifted me. He left me in the straddling position before leaning back with me on top of him. As he did this I automatically adjusted my body to the riding position and got ready to mount his thick rod.

As I sat on his dick, I gasped at the thickness of his girth. I was amazed at how tight my pussy felt as he filled my walls. I steadied myself and then rode him in an up and down motion slowly at first and then with progressing speed. He felt so good inside of me that I thought I would cum instantly. However, just when I thought I would explode, he flipped me over, climbed on top of me, and began thrusting my walls to his own beat.

I closed my eyes and let out a series of uncontrollable moans and then a scream of ecstasy as he rode my pussy. I did not move when he slowed down briefly to grab a toy from the nightstand and turned it on. It made a sweet humming sound as he pushed my legs back and inserted the tip in my anus nice and slow. Very few got the pleasure of fucking my asshole but somehow I did not utter one single protest as he slid it in and out of my rectum with long and deep motions. I let out a small scream before he covered my mouth then ran his massive hands up the entire length of my body before resting them on my neck.

I enjoyed being choked so this did not bother me as he lightly gripped my neck then squeezed tighter and tighter until I felt the air start to close off around me, my head cocked back.

A few seconds later, my eyes popped open and bulged from their sockets along with the veins which I felt now protruding from my fragile neck.

Was this a part of the sex game? If so what was my safety word? These were the things I thought as a fuzzy haze began to surround me and I slowly began losing consciousness.

Chapter 36

Devine

In this lavish hotel suite that I had booked especially for this occasion, I wondered how long she was going to keep up this charade as if she did not know me.

It had been a rocky three months taking care of my brother Gene who had come to stay with me upon his release from the hospital when he came out of his coma. Although my dad had dropped the bombshell of my life on me, I had to turn this thing around and get to know him starting from the very moment I knew that he was my brother. I could no longer live in the past or revel in the time we had lost as siblings. What was done was done. Besides, he did not have much of any other family in the area.

When I found out he had lost memory of the entire incident that led him in the hospital, I was there to ensure he had the proper assistance including physical therapy for what would be a long journey.

I explained to him what he did not know about his paternal family. I learned that he was told by his mother, who had passed a few years ago, that his father was deceased. Although there was no doubt that my father was indeed his father, due to a paternity test I learned they took when he was an infant, the councilman did not choose to step up even now. He was fearful that the media would get a hold of the story and tarnish his reputation.

I was disappointed to say the least because the father I thought I knew was no more and it would take me some time to get over that. In fact I was boiling mad and had refused to take his calls or entertain his visits over the past few months. My mother had tried to reach out to me but I only visited her when I knew he was not around.

But anyways, I kept this game of cat and mouse up from the time I spotted her at the party from across the room. Now, I stared at her beautiful body as she undressed down to her panties and bra and got in the hot tub with me. I continued to play along as we made our way to the bedroom and I lifted her into the straddling position before sitting on the soft king sized bed and allowing her to take control as she rode me like the beautiful stallion that she was.

I did not understand her obsession with anal play but I grabbed the vibrating toy she had placed on the night stand earlier and penetrated her long and deep watching her breathing quicken before she let out an orgasmic scream. As instructed I dominated her asshole hovering over the top of her and using my free hand to cover her mouth as she screamed.

"Choke me" she yelled as soon as I took my hand from her mouth.

"Choke me now" she commanded.

I slowly slid my hands around her neck and applied increasing pressure careful not to squeeze too tight. I wasn't into this kinky shit but whatever made her happy I was bound to oblige.

Besides it was my birthday and maybe I needed to live a little outside of my box. Perhaps that was why she was laying it on extra thick for me now with this mysterious game we started back at the party. This was my first party and with everything that was going on she had suggested that I meet her and Sidney there to experience my first time to such an event with her right there.

She explained that we would not have to engage in anything but rather watch. She assured me it would be a new foreplay experience before we finished my birthday in style at the famous Cartwright hotel.

I can't lie though, at first this invitation surprised me because I had no clue she was into that but I didn't mind much because I loved her and she assured me she had not been since we had gotten serious and that she would not go again without me. Swinging who knew? Besides how could I get angry knowing I was holding secrets of my own including the fact that a woman may be carrying my seed.

"Tighter you whore!" she yelled as I unsuccessfully tried to cater to her wishes.

I knew some women liked to be choked but she had been getting more and more into this submissive stuff lately. I always heard the rule was choke her until she was woozy. That was as far as it should go was what I always told by even her admission when I questioned her about her obsession with this type of play.

However, I noticed as time went on she damn near wanted to pass out before she uttered the safety word "touch" she had come up with early on in our sexual relationship after our first encounter at her place. That was the first night she introduced me to the art of seductive choking. I had actually let her choke me back a few times that night but her grip was strong and it made me uncomfortable as a man so we discontinued that real quick. A short while later I learned she also loved anal play but not the actual act of anal sex.

In a zone now my mind was wandering to those thoughts so I did not notice when she reached under the pillow, uttered a few words, and in one swift motion raised her hand and then.......

Bam!

I had never been shot before so it took me a minute to register the ringing sound that was going off in my head as a warm sensation oozed down the side of my face. The cocking of the gun snapped me back to reality and then the fight was on.

Like a wild woman Jade was struggling beneath me a look of rage and hate quickly spreading across her face as her wig came off revealing her beautiful long dark hair.

"What the fuck" I yelled as I tried to gain control of the weapon she had in her hands.

The woman I loved was far removed as her eyes went stone cold and dark, her skin flushed.

"I hate you" she confirmed flailing and screaming beneath me trying to steady her aim as I fought to knock the gun from her hands. However, she was stronger than I thought and was not giving in.

Her long beautiful hair became a mangled mess strewn about her head as she shook it back and forth violently. I was beginning to feel weak as a fuzzy haze spread across my vision.

"Argggghhh!" I screamed as she raised her head and bit me hard on my left shoulder.

Did I hear her right when she said "Death to you Uncle Ray," blood dripping down the corner of her mouth from the fresh wound she inflicted upon my shoulder?

Lord what is going on?

That was all I could think as I tried to make sense of what was happening and prayed to not pass out before I could diffuse this unexpected turn of events. The burning sensation in my shoulder was only slightly helping with that.

Being in a penthouse suite, I figured the noise we were making would go unheard so I decided to take matters in my own hand as my energy started to succumb to a losing battle.

With my last ounce of strength, I grabbed the gun tight with my left hand while raising my right hand as high as I could, which wasn't very high given the pain. Then with everything in me I punched the love of my life across her beautiful face knocking her out cold.

The struggle beneath me now vanished as I blinked hard. I don't remember calling 9-1-1 before drifting off to a deep sleep filled with the thought of Jade and newfound love now forever lost. Happy Birthday to me.....

Epilogue

Sidney

Sixteen, this was the number assigned to the confirmed body count for our friend Jade Alexander as she sat confined to St. Agnes, a maximum security mental institution in nearby Virginia.

From the time I buried my mom as a girl until now, tragedy and death have long since been a part of my life. However, nothing could prepare me for the recent events or the information that came to light in the weeks following the discovery that the person responsible for terrorizing our nation's capital was one of my closest girlfriends who had long battled mental illness including Schizophrenia and Obsessive-Compulsive disorder for more than half of her life.

She was bound by psychotic episodes that came and went sometimes without warning. Sometimes these episodes were followed by violent outbreaks that she inflicted upon herself and others but no one who knew of her battle felt she was capable of murdering anyone.

We learned that although she was from New Jersey, she had spent a great portion of her adult life in Houston, TX after moving there to attend school for business with her boyfriend Christian.

He had moved there that same year on a full athletic scholarship leaving earlier in the summer to attend camp.

While there in Texas Jade landed an internship, with the help of her father, which equipped her with the knowledge of the art buying business and assisted her in starting her own art gallery. Her father was reluctant at first but because he did not fully understand the magnitude of her illness, he believed that the new environment would actually help her cope and somehow cure her. His rationale was that she would finally be able to live her dreams and do what she wanted to do with her life. Her mother went along with that theory.

It was there in Houston that the bodies of her boyfriend and two women, he was rumored to have cheated on her with, were found in an apartment brutally shot and stabbed to death. Nina saw the special that flashed a picture of her beautiful exotic face as one of the nation's most wanted in connection with those murders as well as murders that had taken place in the states of New Jersey and New York prior.

Nina explained that she had tried numerous time to call me and then Jade as she knew Jade would be able to confirm my location.

Apparently, Jade had moved to the DC area to flee her past. It is unknown what sparked her sexually sadistic murderous spree in the nation's capital but she has been connected to many of the unsolved homicides. In fact, she was formally charged in the murder of the young couple who Nina informed me happen to be the same couple from the party we attended for my birthday.

They were transplants to the area but had been involved in the lifestyle for years having connections in their hometown that hooked them up with our network here in DC. That happened to be their first and last party here as they exchanged information with Jade and met her back at their place after Nina dropped us back off at the metro station.

She was also connected to the Marcel Bennett case as well as the attack of Gene and subsequent murder of his friend all of whom were bi-sexual males. It was unclear if she targeted them because of that fact but it was rumored that someone had seen her having sex with Marcel and a dark skinned gentleman at the Cartwright event. The individual did not see it as being related to the case and was reluctant to come forward until recently when the news broke of her capture.

However, the shock of them all came in the form of the young lady who was found in the dumpster of the alley in SE Washington, DC. Her name was Kim and she happened to be the girl that had been actively pursuing my brother Kenny. He figured she had just gotten the hint and stopped calling him, not having a clue that she was in fact dead. It is unclear how Jade came in contact with her but she was found not far from Kenny's studio in the dumpster of a dark alley. There was nothing to tie her to Kenny so they did not have any reason to question him at the time and so he remained in the dark about her murder never having seen her face on the news.

Furthermore, when authorities entered Jade's home on a search warrant, they found pictures, the cellular number, and address of a lady that was later identified as one of Devine's club members by the name of Mya Neumann hanging on her wall with explicit terms scribbled on the print and holes cut in key unidentified areas of her body. When questioned, Mya admitted to calling Devine's girlfriend anonymously and playing on her phone numerous times but had no idea that Jade was able to gain access to all of her information and was in fact stalking her. The fear by authorities was that she would have been the next victim for reasons that were still not completely known.

With all that has come out, I can't help but wonder if she had anything to do with the shooting of Pete and Kenny although she appeared to adore him. Authorities have not connected her to this incident but it still remains unsolved to date.

As far as Devine is concerned, surprisingly he was only grazed by the bullet from the gun Jade aimed at his head at point blank range. I consider him blessed.

I wondered if I should have saw something in the strange manner in which Jade was acting toward him at the party. I figured they were just spicing up their relationship for his birthday when they pretended to not know each but it did feel quite strange when she felt the need to give me all of his information. Furthermore, she almost looked as if she wanted to protest or she was looking for me to object when they left but I chalked that up to her not wanting to leave me alone at the party.

I felt bad for Devine because I know he really cares for Jade and from what I heard he has been to visit her a few times since he has gotten out of the hospital believing that she loved him too and not faulting her for her illness.

We still keep in touch with him and Nina let me know she plans on sending him an invite to the wedding scheduled to take place next summer between her and Jay.

As the winter months set in I can't help but sit at my bay window from time to time and wonder what went so wrong that one of my best friends would be capable of such heinous acts.

Jade Alexander, a female serial killer the likes of which this city had never seen. I guess mental illness is one of those subjects we dare not discuss until we are forced or somehow tempted to touch.

Breinigsville, PA USA
20 February 2011
255941BV00003B/4/P